AF406538

OUTLAWS PUBLISHING

HONOR BOUND

SCOTT HOWEY

For information contact: info@outlawspublishing.com

Cover Art by Michael Thomas

Cover design by Outlaws Publishing LLC

Published by Outlaws Publishing LLC

May 2024

10987654321

CHAPTER 1

The thud of hooves on the hard earth was monotonous. The rhythmic sound of the horse's gait accompanied the man rolling back and forth in the saddle. It was his fourth day in the saddle, and he was tired. He allowed time to pass him by and found solace when he rode. It was when he stopped that the reason for his swift riding came back to haunt him. But there was a need to stop because the mount was slowing, and he needed to stretch. It was late afternoon and a series of clouds banked to the west. He would be well advised to ensure he hunkered down for the night. The thought ate him up, but he knew it was the right decision. Descending a ridge, he maneuvered between some pines, leaned back in the saddle, and covered the rocky incline, and kicked the mount on. He reached the rise of a small hill and paused. Straight ahead, a quarter of a mile, he saw a fissure in the earth that ran from the hills to his right down the mountainside, through the valley, and snaked its way across the plain. Trees banked the fissure and he acknowledged it for what it was, water. Nudging the chestnut, he covered the distance leisurely and dismounted.

The creek was twenty feet wide and shallow. He could have walked across it without the water going past his knees. Instead, he let the chestnut have its fill while he rolled a smoke. He paced back and forth, struck a match on his belt buckle, and brought the smoke to life. He looked around. At another time, when the man wasn't burdened with sorrow, he might have contemplated its form. It would have appealed to him if he had a mind to reflect on the grassy plains, the rolling hills, and the clear, fresh water, but he was burdened. It was a vow unfulfilled. An oath to a dying mother, uttered when she was both in the land of the living and six-foot under the earth. For twelve months he had scoured the land. He rode north to Winton and south to Aniston. He roamed the rugged peaks of the Windy mountains to the west and rode the vast empty plains to the east. Day and night. He rode with purpose. He chased down lead after lead, but all to no avail. He nearly died of thirst and was attacked by a grizzly, but he survived. He always did. It didn't matter what was thrown his way he always came out on top. He was no gunslinger, but a finer brawler there never was. He wasn't a true shot with a rifle, but he equipped himself well enough for others to take notice. Brett Langford was not to be trifled with.

He unsaddled the horse and hitched it sound. If a storm were to blow, the mount wouldn't pull free. He built a fire and set to work making a shelter to protect himself from the elements. He cut a sapling ten feet long and wedged it in the crook of two trees. He then cut more and made a frame which he interlaced with branches he found on the ground. When he finished, he had made a crude tent, but it was better than nothing.

He sat down before the fire. He put his saddlebags and bedroll under the shelter and sat with his slicker on to warm him against the chill. He pulled the slicker tight and wrapped his arms around himself to keep warm. He recalled his mother just before she passed. The room was dark. His aunty sat in the corner of the room rocking back and forth. She took up lots of room and her weight made both the chair and the floor squeak, but he noticed it only when he thought he noticed the silence. His thoughts were with his mother. She was spindly and pale, but her voice was firm. "Your brother was a good boy son. He always looked up to you since you were little. You know what you have to do."

"I know, Mama."

Her voice was raspy. "Well, what are you waiting for?"

He grabbed his mama by the hand and prayed solemnly. "I'm not going anywhere until the Lord takes you away."

Coraline Langford coughed violently, and he let go of his mother's hand and stood. His aunty moved swiftly for a large woman and sat her sister up and patted her gently on the back. She pointed to her nephew. "Water."

He responded and handed her an enamel mug after he dipped it in a bucket of tepid brown water. "Here."

The woman took it, though it looked as if she wanted to chastise him for something, instead she pulled a fly out of the cup and flicked it at him. It hit him in the cheek. He never liked her. She was always complaining about something. As soon as his ma passed, he would ride away and never see the woman again.

His ma sipped only a little and coughed again before she laid back down on the bed. He moved closer as the big woman pushed past him. He saw a tear in her eye as she passed. Kneeling on the floor, he looked into his mother's eyes one last time before she closed them on the world. She managed three last words. "Promise me, son."

He felt the tears sting his eyes. "I promise, Mama."

She closed her eyes, and her breathing went quiet. She exhaled one last breath and then death descended on the room. He sat with her in silence. The air was heavy and the mood somber.

He felt the rain and lifted his face to the sky. He stared into space for a while, and it was hard to tell if the man had shed more tears. The memory of her passing cleaved itself to his chest. It weighed him down. Removing the slicker, he crawled under his makeshift shelter, folded up the slicker, and used it for a pillow. He tossed the blanket over his legs, made sure his Peacemaker was beside him and then he listened to the rain. It approached like a freight train, feeling its way across the earth with intent.

Brett Langford, the son of Coraline and the brother to Charlie, interred his mother on the afternoon of her death. There were only himself and his aunty in attendance. It was a hasty service, one without pomp and ceremony. Little was said over the woman's broken body, but her firstborn son stood at the foot of her grave with his hat in his hands and swore an oath. "Mama, I promise I will kill the son of a bitch that murdered Charlie."

He would never forget the man's name. No matter how long it took he would hunt his brother's killer down and keep the promise he made to his dying mother. He mounted and rode away, without turning around. If he had, he would have seen his aunty kneeling on the ground with her eyes to the sky. She was praying for her nephew Charlie who was gunned down in the prime of his life. She prayed for her sister who was taken way too soon. She prayed for Brett Langford, the sole male heir to the Langford name. Lastly, she prayed for herself. Her words were masked with sorrow. "Lord, please, don't let me die alone."

CHAPTER 2

Will Lonergan lay in the dust. A bullet in his throat. He pawed helplessly at the wound as blood ran through his fingers and buried itself in the dust. He stared up at a sky that was folding in on him. His world was spinning, death was consuming him, and he was afraid. His time on this earth was at an end and he was having regrets, lots of them. But as so often is the case, it was too late. This is what his life had come to. He couldn't change a damn thing, though just minutes earlier a simple decision could have saved his life.

Will Lonergan was no good. Everything that could be said about a man who sported an undesirable brand was true about the man who lay dying in the street. He was untrustworthy and shiftless. He spent his life slinking from town to town like a coyote and then pouncing on the first morsel that favored his lot in life. His appearance was shabby, and his words were oiled with grease and slipped out too easy. A vow was easily made and broken. The stories he told of his role in the war were fables. They started with 'once upon a times' and always ended with him being the hero. A martyr to the cause.

Thorn Hannon walked casually along the main street of Lewisburg. They knew who he was, though they didn't know much about the man himself, except the rumors. But talk doesn't make a man. It can break him, but it sure as hell doesn't make him. Though the man who walked was the same boy that left Lewisburg years earlier, he wasn't the same who returned. A lot happened in a short time. A person learns to grow. He moves with the punches and doesn't grow roots until he is of a mind to consider such a life prosperous. They all knew the reason he came back, not one of them mentioned it to him, but they all knew. In many ways, the conflict that ensued moments before was nearly a year in the making. It festered underneath the surface and lay dormant. The men were bound to clash. Why it happened on this day no one knew for sure, but it was as good a day as any, to die.

Hannon was tall, wide, and square of shoulder. His face was set in an almost permanent frown. His jaw square and firm. It was a moody look, but the man was pensive. His stride slowed and he lowered the rifle as he approached. He watched Lonergan as he began making strange noises and his legs began jerking involuntarily. Hannon looked to his left and right, stopped, and turned the full circle. He was wary of interlocutors, however, he suspected that the spectators knew who was gasping for air, and they wouldn't be overly concerned. No one came to the dying man's aid. He held his rifle in his right hand while his left caressed the barrel. It was a Winchester.73, a little worse for wear, but it fired true. It was his bread and butter. It had been for some time, and he nurtured it like a cow does its calf. He made eye contact with them all. His experience as a lawman hundreds of miles north was evident in his cautious yet firm approach. His senses were alert. Every sound sharp. His manner dared strangers to challenge him. They needed to know that Thorn Hannon wasn't to be trifled with.

He took another step towards the dying man, and satisfied he was safe from the gathering hoard, let his eyes fall on the soon to be carcass of Lonergan. He considered the man briefly. His presence and his past. Lonergan, according to the life he scripted for himself, was a war hero, gunslinger, and all-round Casanova. "Hah," he spat into the street at the thought of it. The words escaped him involuntarily. "More like, murderer."

He had seen many dying men and the scene was always the same. Folks gathered to stare, occasionally a woman fainted, a man would curse, and a hush would descend upon the onlookers. Lonergan was dying, no doubt about it, Thorn could hear the man gurgling and choking on his blood. Thorn lowered his rifle and pointed it at his victim.

"You're done for, I've seen to it."

At the sound of Thorn's voice, Lonergan looked towards his killer. His eyes clouded in mist, his life fading slowly. He knew he was done for; knew he was dying and he was scared.

Thorn looked him in the eye and said "answer one question and I'll make your journey into hell quick, lie and I'll make it slow and painful. Do you understand?"

Despite the wound, Will bloody Lonergan managed to nod his acceptance. It was slow and painful, but it was there.

Thorn asked the next question, slowly but with venom. "Did you shoot Wade; my brother?" Wade was found dead on his spread south of Lewisburg a year earlier. Two gunshot wounds in the back.

Wade was a tough man, not a gunslinger, but a tough man. His fists had scarred Will Lonergan's face and a permanent scar over the dying man's left eye was a reminder of the day he dared to paw Elizabeth, Wade's wife. On that fateful day, revenge sat heavy in Will's mind and Wade Hannon had unknowingly sealed his fate. A month later he was found dead.

Thorn looked at the dying man and said, "just because you're the sheriff's little brother it doesn't mean you can break the law and it certainly doesn't mean you're made of steel." Wade had proven that!

The dying man looked at his killer, and with greater effort than before nodded his acceptance. Thorn stood upright, back straight, and scanned the crowd. "Did everybody see that?" A voice from his right said, "I did, he just admitted to killing your brother. A mighty fine man he was. Yes, sir, a mighty fine man." It was McGee, the general store owner.

"I saw it", shouted Thompson, the town barber. The faces started nodding in agreement with the two men.

They all agreed that Will Lonergan admitted to murdering Wade Hannon. The lonely figure on the ground contorted and twisted as he coughed up the crimson liquid.

Thorn lifted his rifle and aimed it at the man's chest and before he sent him to hell he said: "It's more than you deserve." The bullet thudded into his chest, surprisingly it left little evidence of its impact.

"Someone find the Sheriff", yelled Marlowe, the fat and smelly barkeep. Thorn raised his head and eyeballed the man. Marlowe tried to stare back, but he couldn't hold the gaze. Thorn saw the fear in his eyes and made a gesture towards him as if he were next. Marlowe turned and ran, his true colors shining through. Yellow to the core.

The crowd laughed which eased the tension. McGee said, "the sheriff's out of town on official business, the deputy and mayor went with him, I saw them heading north about sunrise."

"When's he due back?" asked Peaty with a slur. He had no liking for the sheriff. It seemed he got locked up far too much for simply falling asleep whenever he was tired, or drunk.

"Marlowe will know," said the undertaker as he made his way through the crowd to the corpse, gesturing to some men to carry the body. As the men left, he turned and faced Thorn, he looked him up and down, out of interest, perhaps thinking that his tall and wide frame would need an extra size pine box. He said in a matter-of-fact voice, "it seems that Marlowe always knows where the sheriff is and what he's doing".

Thorn saw a glimpse of derision in the undertaker's eye. Not for himself, but for Marlowe and the sheriff.

A female voice from the back of the crowd asked plaintively, "Why would the mayor go with the sheriff on official business?" Though the crowd had started to break up and the noise drowned out her question, Thorn heard it and figured he already knew the answer to the question.

CHAPTER 3

Thanks to Mayor Lloyd Ellery, Lewisburg was a small town with a big city attitude. It was a cauldron of discontent and he was the instigator. He had been mayor for eighteen months and had done a fine job of dividing the townsfolk in two. Those willing to accept change and those who weren't. This discontent was the source of much discussion and disharmony. Arguments erupted on the steps of the church, on the main street of town, and in the saloons. Everyone had an opinion, and few were willing to budge. It was as if there were only two choices and people had to choose either way. Those without an opinion were few. They were content to live their life as best they knew and considered it a waste of time worrying either way. Lifelong friendships splintered and even husbands and wives found that disharmony and division crept into their homes. It was a tumultuous time, one in which few people prospered.

The first consisted of business folk and their kin, of course, money their priority. There were two exceptions to this, and they were Thompson, the barber, and McGee, the store owner. They were of an age and in a position where they were content with their lot in life and wanted their grandchildren to have the same lifestyle they had experienced. Looking back through the lens of age a person often recalls the innocence of youth. It was a world without complications. It was such a world that

Thompson and McGee wanted, not only for their children and grandchildren but for all the residents of Lewisburg. In private, they had conceded to one another that the wheels of change had too much traction, and the world they pined for was long gone. However, they also agreed that something worth believing in is worth fighting for.

The rest of the business interests openly supported the mayor. Progress was their cry, but money was their cause. They turned a blind eye to what they saw and a deaf ear to the rumors. If they could benefit, that was all that mattered.

Ellery was a man of words. He was swift of movement and tongue. His talk was glib and his wit sharp. He was a thinker, he was a man of script, not action. For that he paid others. He spoke quickly and his voice was sickly sweet. He was everything the folks of Lewisburg were not. Men of the man's ilk had passed through town on the stage and stayed a night or two, but Ellery had brought his wife and decided to call the place home. As soon as his foot hit the dust of the main street after alighting from the stage, he began asserting his influence. He was small in stature, but he wore it well. Some develop their status because of their deeds or inherit it by birth, but the most powerful were those who had it simply because of their wealth. He was such a man.

Some took a liking to him because he told them what they wanted to hear, and others couldn't get far enough away from him. To these people, Ellery couldn't be trusted. Besides, they liked the easy-going lifestyle Lewisburg had developed. It was in danger of disappearing forever and they didn't like it one bit. It just so happened that they were in the minority. They questioned the credentials of the man from the east who turned up overnight in Lewisburg three years earlier. He was the antagonist. He talked of the railroad and how it's inevitable surge north would swallow the country. Ellery called it a technological age, an awakening. A moment in history where mankind would make great leaps forward. He was an articulate and brisk character who sported a thin mustache. He had a habit of running his right hand down his shirt front and playing with the buttons, while he spoke. He was a true champion of the cause for change, and he had some powerful allies such as Dobbins, the banker. The latter was as important as they come and head of Lewisburg's Chamber of Commerce. Ellery thought he had Dobbins fooled. Ellery spoke of life back east and the fancy and finery of such a lifestyle. The music, the arts, and the fashion were great topics at dinner parties of which he was the center of attention. Politics was a staple topic of conversation. So too was economic growth and expansion. For some, it was a romantic time. For others, a time for sorrow. The future had never seemed so close, the past a distant memory. It all seemed far away but the prospect of it all was real enough. His wife played her part and did so with alacrity. It didn't take long for his supporters to understand the message and it was simply that the railroad meant jobs in its construction, it also meant people, and people equaled money.

For the railroad to pass through town, the community needed to be united. A single message needed to be sent to congress that Lewisburg was prepared to be at the forefront of change. However, Ellery had his agenda, as people do, and this involved buying land and lots of it. He had managed through sheer cunning, both legal and illegal maneuvering, and a few accidental deaths, to acquire more than his fair share of land, north, and east of the town. It was the land that lay south-west of Lewisburg and west of the Canyon River as it wove its way north that eluded him. Over twenty thousand acres of prime grazing land lay in the hands of two families. The McKinnon's and the Hannon's. If the railroad passed through Lewisburg, which he truly doubted, the McKinnon and Hannon land would be of no use to him as it was too far out of the way, but he wanted to own it because he liked to possess things, this includes people and institutions. Even the law.

CHAPTER 4

It was in the morning on the day that his brother was killed in the main street of Lewisburg that Sheriff Lonergan and Deputy Slick Jones escorted the mayor to the McKinnon spread. It was a warm morning. They rode side by side with Ellery in the middle, the sheriff to his left, and the deputy to his right. They crested a rise eleven miles south of town when the mayor's thoughts were interrupted.

"It sure is quiet out here," uttered the sheriff. He could only stand silence for so long. It made him uncomfortable. The mayor and Slick Jones cherished the silence. The mayor because it gave him time to think about what had to be done and who he could exploit to ensure his financial interests were secure. Slick Jones liked the silence because although he had a fondness for people, he liked to escape them occasionally.

It was the deputy who replied to the statement. "It was."

The sheriff laughed. He liked Slick Jones, well used to is probably more apt. According to Ellery, Jones had become an impediment to their plans. A man as honorable as the small deputy had been a hindrance in the past and no doubt would be again. He was only along because of the man's ability with his Colt. No other reason. The mayor demanded protection and there was no better man for the job, than Slick Jones.

The men halted on a rise a mile from the McKinnon spread. It was ten thousand acres of the finest grazing land in the county. The land was fertile and the beef they passed, though few, marked with the McKinnon brand, were healthy. The grass, either side of the track that led to the ranch house, was knee-high. It swayed gently in the breeze. The mood was inviting, though the intent of the visit was less so. Sheriff Lonergan had recalled many such visits to ranches around Lewisburg. They didn't always go to plan, but in the end, one of two things happened. The rancher sold or they were met with an accident that resulted in death. In the ensuing mess, Ellery would always end up the legal owner of the land in question. He would prefer to buy it outright. It was easier that way. In the end, the mayor always got what he wanted, and the sheriff was helping the man do it.

Lonergan was once a prideful man, but that seemed so long ago. He respected the law he swore to uphold, but Ellery had found some chinks in the man's morality. He was aging and the day when he was incapable of performing his regular duties was fast-approaching. He was also broke. Both circumstances fostered a need and the man called Ellery was willing to help him satisfy that need, however, all things come at a price. In the end, Lonergan decided that his needs were more important than the lives of the citizens he had sworn to protect. He slept easy at night even though the differences between right and wrong became harder for him to understand and identify. He had become slovenly in his duty and his appearance. The beginning of his downfall began years earlier. It was a year before Ellery turned up in town. His brother Will Lonergan drifted into Lewisburg. He had spent his time since the war drifting aimlessly. He was like many men after the conflict, who found it difficult to call a place home. He was worthless and shifty and he, as he always did, rubbed off on his older brother. The lawman had become weak-willed and his fall from grace was evident to the folks that elected him Sheriff, but he wouldn't win another term. The people had decided that his time had come.

The house and surrounding buildings sat, nestled in the valley. Beyond the McKinnon spread, the holding was Hannon's ranch. The Pike Mountains to the south loomed majestically in the distance.

"Do you reckon she'll sell?" asked the mayor.

Sheriff Lonergan lifted his hat and wiped his brow, somewhat nervous about the pending conversation with Sarah McKinnon. He knew her well enough and though he had never had much to do with the McKinnon clan he spoke as if he did. "I don't see why she won't. Her Ma died last spring and she's been struggling ever since."

Ellery smiled. "That's what I like to hear. Yes, sir, today is going to be a good day."

Ellery hadn't been in Lewisburg for a week when he approached Sheriff Edward Lonergan and made his intentions clear. He bought the lawman's loyalty. The lawman was slowing down and didn't have long left. His campaign as Sheriff was successful the previous year only because of Ellery's and Dobbin's influence. They were like-minded men and Lonergan thought himself their equal, but he was wrong. Men like Ellery and Dobbins had no equals. They surround themselves with fools when they have a need, and they have a need. But Ellery was dependent on Dobbins. As rich as he was, he would need the banks backing to move on the land. He hated being in such a position, but he was wise enough to understand that acquiring wealth could be a lengthy process. There were times to speculate and there were times to plan, and he was doing both.

As they approached the ranch Slick Jones observed the great stack of firewood, noticed how the corral was well mended, the barn looked to be in good shape and there was even a vegetable garden near the outhouse. "It doesn't look like she's doing it tough," mumbled Slick Jones.

Just as the mayor was about to utter his agreement the door of the house opened, and a young woman stepped onto the porch. She was tall, not overly, and quite skinny, but any man could tell she was more than capable of looking after herself.

"No need to dismount, I expect that you won't be here long," she uttered confidently.

The sheriff leaned forward in his saddle, took off his hat, and wiped his brow again. "Now, Miss. McKinnon, may I call you Sarah?"

"I'd prefer it if you didn't, it'll be Miss. McKinnon to you." She took a step closer, rubbed her hands together, held them out in front of her, and said: "well, let's hear it."

Before the sheriff uttered another word, the mayor spoke up. "Miss. McKinnon, it's a nice place you have here." He waited for a reply, but none was forthcoming. She just looked at him as if to say hurry up. "Alright, Miss. McKinnon, since you seem to prefer a direct conversation, I'll come straight out with it."

"I'd prefer it, got things to do."

The Mayor was put off by her attitude and took a moment to gather his thoughts and said, "I'll give you three dollars an acre."

"Not for sale, you are wasting your time, you should leave now."

Sheriff Lonergan went to speak but the mayor raised his hand to stop him. "Four dollars an acre."

"Mister, you must be deaf, I said this place isn't for sale." There was a defiant tone in her voice.

Sheriff Lonergan said, "it must be lonely out here Miss. McKinnon, a woman of your class should be back east when she could live a life of leisure. Imagine the life you could live with all that money," blabbered the sheriff.

She tilted her head to the left and stared at him. She didn't say a word.

"Five dollars……." the mayor was cut off.

"Regardless of your offer," she said, "I have been made a better one."

The mayor was puzzled, and his words came out quick, "how is that possible?"

Sarah could tell the man they called the mayor was getting frustrated. She felt the tension rise and as she turned to leave, she said, "you need to speak to Mr. Hannon." As she turned, she paused and gave Slick Jones an inquiring look, wiped her hands on her apron, went back inside and closed the door.

CHAPTER 5

The men rode in silence. The mayor was angry. He was moving around in the saddle and fidgeting with his attire. They were sure signs the man was uncomfortable. Miss. McKinnon's abruptness caused him some concern as he contemplated the next course of action. Her refusal was blunt, and no amount of negotiating was going to change her mind. Ellery had been around long enough to know the nature of such things. Still, the woman's words were uncompromising. He felt an intense dislike for her and considered her arrogant and dismissive. He felt her rejections as sharply as he heard her words. She had pluck and it was a trait he admired but at this moment in time, he felt it more of a hindrance than anything else.

Each man felt the mood shift but didn't give voice to it. They wore it on their shoulders like a cloak, a heavy cloak. It was only the mayor who was burdened by Sarah McKinnon's words. His companions were lost in their contemplations.

Sheriff Lonergan was working up the courage to demand the money that was owed to him. Lonergan was promised a hundred dollars for his help in securing the Wilson spread a month earlier. Wilson owned a large spread fifteen miles north of Lewisburg, west of the road leading north that ran parallel with the Canyon River. He met with an untimely accident and the deed to his property ended up in the hands of Lloyd Ellery. The land was fair and of reasonable value, enough that he would make a profit on it. The lawman suddenly became angry. A man as rich as Ellery sure was slow in paying his debts.

Ellery was quick to promise and slow on coming through at his end. But men who wear the same shade end up finding one another eventually. They share the same traits and possess the same thoughts. A man can start with honorable intentions, but through circumstances lean a completely different way. It was that way with the sheriff. Ellery, well, he had always leaned a little. Men of the mayor's and the sheriff's ilk quite often overestimated their hand. Their minds worked overtime. They ran through every scenario in their minds. It was like a movie reel on loop. Such men found rest only when they were content, and Ellery was anything but pleased with what transpired. He couldn't keep the conversation with Miss. McKinnon out of his mind. He didn't think she'd be so hostile. He underestimated her. Something he doesn't normally do. Well, he won't make the same mistake twice. What did she mean when she said, "talk to Mr. Hannon?" What did he have to do with her? It was a problem he didn't want to have to deal with. Not yet. Thorn Hannon turned up a month after his brother's death. No one knew where he had been before this. There were rumors of course but Ellery, though he found them interesting, didn't put much faith in them.

The rumor mill had him fighting Indians in Arizona, in prison in Wyoming, and driving cattle in Texas. The great cattle rush was on and the markets, though far away, were paying top dollar. There was work to be had in Texas for the adventurous. Life wasn't always easy, but it suited a particular man, and most folks considered Thorn Hannon the type. There was even one suggestion, though it was strong in its determination, and that is that Hannon was pushing up daisies. When he rode into town eleven months ago, a month after his brother's death, it was the biggest surprise of all. Ellery didn't particularly care where Hannon had come from. He just wanted him gone.

It was his plan that led to Wade Hannon's demise. He may not have pulled the trigger, but he was just as responsible, and it would be in his bests interests to make sure that Thorn Hannon never found out. Ellery decided that Wade was to have an accident and in consultation with the Sheriff and his brother, Will Lonergan, the latter agreed to arrange it for a nominal fee of two hundred dollars. It was all Wade Hannon's life was worth. The problem was that two bullets in the back can barely be classed as an accident. Drowning or falling off a cliff would have been more palatable to the locals then such a death as Will Lonergan dished out. The mayor had learned his lesson and another rancher who refused to sell, Wilson, was disposed of judiciously and appropriately. It involved confiding in and working closely with a select few. It is just that there had been some cracks appearing of late and he needed to stem the tide before it was too late.

Wade's wife, Elizabeth heard the shooting and ran outside to see a man on a bay disappearing through the morning mist. She wrote a letter to her brother-in-law who promptly returned. Not long after, Elizabeth returned to Baxter to live with her parents. Before she left, the spread was sold to Thorn. Where he got the money from was a source of gossip for the locals, however, he became the legal and outright owner of over twelve thousand acres of prime land. The notion didn't sit well with Ellery, but the death of Hannon's brother was still too fresh in the minds of the locals to make a move on the land, just yet.

Greed has its place, but greed accompanied with stupidity was a foolish combination. He should have owned the land by now, but the mongrel Will Lonergan had spoiled his plans.

Wade Hannon was respected by the locals. He caused no disfavor and spoke ill of no man. His temper was fair, and his mind was set. He had little inclination to mind the affairs of others and preferred a simple life on the land than the back-alley gossip that seems to infect lots of folks. He was happily married and expecting his first child when he was gunned down in cold blood. When Lonergan tried to get amorous with Mrs. Hannon, the farmer, dealt out his brand of punishment. When he finished the bloody and unconscious figure of the self-proclaimed war hero lay in the middle of the road. When Wade was murdered the townsfolk had their suspicions but there was no evidence to suggest otherwise.

To the mayor, who considered himself a fair judge of character, it was obvious that Thorn wasn't a farmer. He didn't walk or talk like a man who had spent his life on the land. There was an edge to him that suggested he would be able to manage any challenge thrown his way. He didn't wear a gun, but he felt as if the man didn't need to. He garnered his peer's respect and they spoke highly of him. The man's presence disturbed him. It was Thorn's property that he had in mind to buy after he bought the McKinnon spread. They were neighbors and together the land was worth a pretty penny. He didn't care if the railroad came through town or not. He wanted to own land because land meant money and money meant power. It made sense that the more land a person owned the more powerful, respected, and influential they were. He was mulling his thoughts over when he was interrupted by Slick Jones.

"Dust, someone's riding fast."

Slick Jones moved his hand to the piece that sat comfortably on his hip.

"It's Marlowe' mumbled the sheriff.

"How can you be sure?" asked the deputy.

"His horse, it's the biggest horse I've ever seen, it's the only one strong enough to carry his weight." The sheriff dismounted and waited for the arrival of his friend. The deputy and mayor stayed put. The mayor went back to thinking about what Miss. McKinnon had said. A minute later Marlowe reined his horse to a stop ten yards from them. He was panting and had a hard time catching his breath. Seeing the concern in his face the mayor jumped off his horse and together he and the sheriff waited impatiently for the man to speak.

"Sheriff," he stuttered, wary of the man's reaction, he looked nervously from man to man and eventually worked up the courage and said, "your brother is dead."

The men didn't see Slick Jones smile.

CHAPTER 6

Sheriff Lonergan's voice was tired. It was the third time he had asked Marlowe to repeat the series of events that transpired earlier in the day. "Tell me again what happened, I've got to get the story straight".

Marlowe was sitting across the desk from the sheriff in his office. The barkeep didn't have many friends and he was happy to be the center of attention, even in such trying circumstances. He didn't like Will Lonergan, but he would never let on. It was his best friend's kid brother. He would make the most of the opportunity. He didn't protest the retelling of the story and responded admirably.

Marlowe's place, the Dusty Boot Saloon, was across the street from the law office. It was a dirty joint with its clientele being of a particular breed of man. The locals knew the man and the place well enough to stay away, but there were a few who considered them both, that is the man and the saloon, to their liking. It was a rough place and many a nose had been broken and lots of blood had been spilled within its walls. The whores were past their prime, but no one cared much about it. The Dusty Boot reflected the proprietor, and it couldn't be said that it was a place of cleanliness and class.

Sheriff Lonergan slammed a fist on the table. "Well, don't keep me waiting, get on with it."

Startled, Marlowe began to recite the events that had transpired the morning before. "I was sweeping the front steps when Will came through the batwings, you know how he liked to drink early in the morning. He must have been drinking all night because he smelt of whiskey. He saw Thorn Hannon who was over by the general store loading supplies onto the wagon. He had that look in his eye. You know, the one he gets when he gets set on a course of action."

"I know."

"He hitched his belt and he straightened his back. His hand fell to his gun and just before he drew, he called out, Thorn Hannon, it's time you and I had a word".

The sheriff interrupted Marlowe, "are you sure those were his exact words?"

"I'm positive that's what he said, McGee was helping Thorn load the wagon, he can verify it."

The sheriff just grunted and waved his hand and said, "go on."

Marlowe took a swig from a mug of cold coffee before he continued. "Well, Hannon put a bag of flour he was carrying on the wagon and turned around to Will holding a gun on him. Thorn wasn't wearing a sidearm. He just stared at your brother for a moment and climbed onto the wagon."
"Just like that?"
"I've never seen a man so calm."

"What happened next?"

"Will shot a bullet over Thorn's head."

"Was he shooting at him?" Interrupted the sheriff.

"I think he was trying to scare him, but Thorn didn't look scared." Marlowe took another drink of coffee. "Thorn walked towards Will. Your brother just stood there with the gun in his hand and he fired over Thorn's head again, but Thorn just kept on walking. He walked straight up to Will and punched him clean on the jaw. Will crumbled to the ground, stunned."

"Huh", the sheriff responded, "he never could take a punch."

Marlowe looked bemused at the comment; however, he continued his story. "Thorn walked back to his wagon and climbed aboard. As he took the reins in his hand Will stumbled to his feet and fired twice, one missed altogether and the other hit the buckboard right beside Thorn. Well, as quick as a coyote in a hen house he reached beside him, the next thing you know he had a rifle in his hands. He stood up and fired one shot that hit your brother in the neck."

Lonergan exhaled deeply, ran his fingers through his hair, rose from his chair, and walked to the door. "Are you sure he fired once?"

"Yes sir", Marlowe said dejectedly.

Through the window of the Sheriff's Office, the last-surviving Lonergan watched the townsfolk go about their business. Mrs. Brady, who owned the haberdashery store, was conversing with Miss. Williams about her pending nuptials. Thompson was sitting on a chair reading, a regular habit of his when times were slow. Peaty was asleep underneath the saloon stairs, no doubt drunk again. He was silent for a moment longer before asking "I suspect that there are plenty of witnesses to back up this story Marlowe?"

"Yes sheriff, most folks saw it, self-defense they are calling it. Hard to argue with them."

"And you say that before he died, he admitted to killing Wade?

"Correct, most folks saw and heard that too."

"Okay Marlowe, I don't care to hear anymore. Seems I'll be unable to arrest him, but I'd still like to bring him in for questioning."

Marlowe nodded approval.

"Keep an ear out, if you hear anything let me know."

Marlowe shook his friend's hand and patted him on the shoulder as he walked through the door, down the steps, across the street, and into the saloon. He said a few words to Peaty who was lying underneath the saloon steps before waddling through the batwings.

The sheriff paced the floor for a while before setting in his chair and placing his feet on the table. He rolled a smoke and drained the last of Marlowe's coffee. He was deep in thought when the mayor startled him.

The mayor looked at the Sheriff coldly, without a care for his brother's death and said, "I'm sorry your brother's dead sheriff, but we have work to do."

Lonergan knew it was a lie, the mayor didn't like Will; not many people did, but he was his brother, and revenge would be assured. Thorn Hannon must die!

Ellery waited impatiently for a reply. "Well, aren't you going to say anything?"

Lonergan shrugged his shoulders, leaned back in his chair, eyeballed the man, and said, "you owe me a hundred dollars."

CHAPTER 7

Ellery stepped into the office and was about to discuss the Sheriff's obvious displeasure with him when Lonergan stood and moved towards the window. Through the wide window, stained with dirt, he could see two men walking across the road and heading for the jailhouse. Thorn Hannon and McGee walked side by side. The man on the left was tall in contrast to the store owner, who was short and spry in comparison. Ellery watched the lawman and moved uncomfortably. His gaze fell on McGee who was a formidable opponent. He didn't have the oratory skill of the mayor, but he was courageous enough to be outspoken, besides he had the support of nearly half the citizenry. He was wise enough to take notice. The other man had been on his thoughts most of the day. Though he had never met the man in question, he awaited the opportunity to do so.

"Looks like you have company, Sheriff."

Lonergan walked back to his desk and waited for the arrival of the man who killed his brother. Ellery moved along the wall and stood motionless. The visitors stepped through the door, with Ellery in the lead. They paused and looked at the mayor before settling their eyes on the lawman. McGee went to speak, but Hannon placed a hand on his shoulder and stepped forward. "Sheriff."

"Hannon. I've been wanting to speak to you." He pointed to the chair and said a little too forcefully, "sit." Hannon eyed him seriously but turned his attention to the mayor who stiffened under Hannon's terse scrutiny. "This doesn't concern you. Leave."
Ellery was lost for words and when he managed to find some, he was cut short. "I have a right."
"You have no right to be here." He then looked at Lonergan. "Either he leaves, or I do."

The mayor pointed at McGee. "What about him?"

"He's a witness."

Ellery tried again but Hannon focused on the man on the other side of the desk. "I will walk."

The sheriff knew he was serious. He had known enough about the Hannon's to realize they meant what they said. He cast a wary glance to the mayor who tried his best to remain in control. Ellery looked pleadingly at him and Lonergan felt a dislike for the man and took the opportunity to use his influence against him and pointed to the door. "You can leave now, Lloyd. This is official law business and is of no concern to you."
Ellery was mad as hell. He glared at the sheriff and then the men who entered and back to the lawman. How dare the sheriff call him by his first name? He took offense and made a mental note to talk to him about it later. Ellery marched out of the office and looked over his shoulder as he crossed the street and headed for home.

Lonergan chuffed. Ellery acted like a spoiled child. "What do you want, Thorn?"

Hannon finally sat. "I saw Marlowe ride out of town earlier today, so I figure you know what happened."

"I do."

"What did he tell you?"

"That you killed Will in self-defense."

McGee who had been quiet stepped forward with a piece of paper in his hand and handed it to the Sheriff. "This is my sworn statement about what happened. Down the bottom are the signatures of seven men and women who witnessed your brother's untimely passing. They and I are committed to testifying in a court of law if Hannon is charged."

He leaned back in the chair. His nerves were on edge and he was getting a headache. He didn't want to be there. He rolled himself a quirley and felt himself relax a little as he exhaled a thick cloud of smoke. He eyed McGee, "Hannon won't be charged. It was a clear case of self-defense." The words hurt, but there was nothing else for him to do.

This time it was Hannon's turn to speak. "He also admitted to killing Wade. It's in the letter."

"The records will be amended to show just that."

Both men were relieved, but McGee was a lot more animated about it. Well then, we will take our leave.

"Come on Thorn, this is cause for celebration. Let's have a drink."

"You go ahead. I want to talk to the sheriff alone." McGee stood beside Hannon and pleaded. "I'm not sure that's a good idea."
"I'll be fine. I won't be long."
The look on his face was incredulous and he stepped backward. "Well, if you're sure."
"I'm sure."
When McGee left the room Hannon leaned forward in his chair. "Get it off your chest, Sheriff."

He began to distance himself from his brother. The words were easy to come by. "Will was no good, Thorn. I just figured he would be shot one day. He had it coming. He made his move and paid the ultimate price."

Lonergan was tied. He felt the weight of the world on his shoulders and knew he couldn't handle it anymore. When he first heard that his brother was killed it was only natural that anger took seed in him and the man had plotted revenge. But after Marlowe relayed the message again and again, he became consumed with a nonchalance. It was as if he didn't care. He felt no sorrow. He felt nothing except tiredness.

"Are you figuring on something like revenge, Sheriff?"
Lonergan felt an honesty overcome him. It was born of another time and place when the man knew who he was and was content with being so. It was a time when not

only the law, but life meant something to him. Life had a purpose and he was someone to be admired. He couldn't figure out exactly what caused him to change, but as he sat across from the man who killed his brother and looked him in the eye, he knew he held no revenge in his heart. He wanted to, but just couldn't. The man he had become was unworthy. He felt hopeless, shook his head in disgust and when he spoke his words were barely audible

"I'd be lying if I didn't say I'd like to give you a licking, but that's as far as it goes. I ain't set on revenge, though barely five minutes ago I swore myself to it. I ain't got time for it, or the nerve. I am getting old, Thorn. My time as Sheriff of Lewisburg is ending. I'd just as soon keep my peace and ride out my time with as little fuss as possible."

Thorn nodded, but he was cautious. Hannon had learned years before that while you listen to what a man says it is just as important to think of all the things he didn't say.

There comes a time in a man's life when the energy and interest he invested in the world comes to pass. It fades because experience has taught him that despite his determination there is only so much he can do to make the world a better place. He does not see the change that he has made because his picture is too large. If he pays attention to those around him then all the good he has done is plain to see. It is in the way he speaks and in turn, is spoken to. It is in the eyes of those that admire, respect, and love him. The sheriff was such a man. He learned his place in the world and was content to play his role as best he could. The townsfolk respected him. His daughter once held him in high regard and doted over him. But something happened. She had changed because he had changed. It wasn't Ellery, nor was it his brother. His attitude shifted before they turned up in Lewisburg. They hastened his freefall into obscurity because that is exactly where he was headed. He had given up on himself and as a man influences those around him positively, he can have the opposite effect. His daughter had changed. She spoke ill of him and challenged his position. Likewise, the town folk's view of him was of a murmuring disregard. The worst thing of all was that he knew it and until that moment in time, didn't care. It is often the death of a loved one that causes a person to reflect on their lives. For most, the feeling is temporary, for a few, life changing. Perhaps, it was time for him to step aside. He was nothing but the mayor's puppet and all he had to show for it was a cheapened view of himself. He had fallen short of his expectations. There comes a moment when a man must decide to yield to time itself or face the consequences of his ignorance. Lonergan had read the signs and it was a sharp learning curve.

Thorn Hannon stood. "I'm sorry it had to come to this sheriff, but I'm glad Wade has finally been brought some justice."

The lawman nodded and couldn't look Hannon in the eye.

The latter made his exit and as he walked through the door, he looked over his shoulder and paused. Behind the desk was a man whose fall from grace had been high enough that he would never recover from the impact. Hannon felt a sudden tinge of sadness for the man and as he stepped into the evening, he shook his head in disbelief and said aloud, "isn't it something when a man can't hold his head up any longer?"

CHAPTER 8

Ellery lived in a double story house on the edge of town. It sat atop a gentle rise as the road headed east for Darville. It was the second-largest house in town, behind that of Dobbins the banker. Ellery, still seething about what happened in the law office moments earlier, uttered a few profanities, and hastily poured himself a drink. Moving across to the opposite side of the room he took a seat by the window. He yawned slightly and drew back the curtains so he could get a clearer view of the street below. It was dark outside and an array of lights, scattered along the street gave a curious insight into the proceedings that were unfolding in one part of Lewisburg. A wagon rolled past, and he could hear its wheels rattle across the earth. It turned right into the main street and disappeared. The road that ran magnetic north out of town wound its way fifty miles ahead to a settlement named Lawnton. The place was a ramshackle collection of hastily constructed abodes, including a saloon, that sat in the middle of a rock-strewn country. The land was harsh and bare and those that called the place home were of a breed suited to such conditions.

Lewisburg was the largest town for the next two hundred miles. North of the town the earth turned barren and water became scarce. It was the nature of the land. The McKinnon and Hannon spread signaled the last of the great soil east of the Canyon River. He was going to own it. Miss McKinnon had complicated things by suggesting he talk with Mr. Hannon. In the end, it didn't change the plan that much, after all, Wilson had refused as well, and he ended up dying in a fire. He could easily have them killed, however, there had been too many suspicious deaths lately and he thought another one, especially if he moved on the land straight away would do him more harm than good. It could jeopardize everything he had worked for.

The townsfolk would begin to ask questions, especially about his association with the Sheriff. Miss. McKinnon's refusal to let go of the land had puzzled him. For some reason, he thought she would sell up and do what the sheriff suggested, head east and live a life of leisure. She had no relatives, was rarely seen in town and it could be said that she didn't have close associates at all, except it seems Thorn Hannon. As far as he was concerned it only prolonged the inevitable. His main concern was Mr. Hannon. He had kept to himself the past year, however, he had gunned down the sheriff's brother that morning. He opened the window to let in some fresh air, leaned back in his chair and closed his eyes.

He headed west with the money he embezzled from his father-in-law, William Tyler. Tyler was a railroad magnate. He had plenty of money and the years Ellery spent working for him as an accountant meant that he was able to embezzle quite a sum. He was confident that the old man would never find out. He was clever enough not to get caught, though that didn't stop him from looking over his shoulder from time to time. Tyler was ferocious and loud. He smoked cigars, wore fancy suits, and lots of jewelry. He had what Ellery wanted, besides, he suffered at the hands of the man's pointed humiliation. He concocted a scheme and funneled money into a special account. It took years, but when he couldn't take the man's taunts any longer, he and his wife packed up and left without a word. His name change from Bennett to Ellery was an extra safeguard against detection. His wife would follow him to the end of the earth. She was dutiful and obedient. The choice between husband and father was an easy one to make. The latter was demanding and hostile. He found fault with her each time they passed one another. Her husband, on the other hand, wanted nothing more than an adornment, with wit, intelligence, and personality. She was willing to play the part. For that, she would be provided with the lifestyle that such a role commissioned. It was a mutual arrangement and one he thought she was content with.

He sipped his scotch absentmindedly. He had money, lots of money, but he wanted more. He acquired the Wilson spread north of town thanks to the sheriff and his dead brother, but it was dry, hard land. Good for nothing dirt, not fit for burying.

"Care for a refill?" Margaret, his wife, stood beside him with the bottle and he held out the glass to accept the gesture.

"I will not waste any more money on dirt, I want the soil along the Canyon River." He was speaking aloud, trying to organize his thoughts. "Miss. McKinnon said talk to Mr. Hannon so that is exactly what I'll do."

"This Thorn Hannon," his wife paused, "I have seen him, the Sheriff and Slick Jones are no match for him."

He turned to her and explored the meaning in her eyes. "What are you suggesting?"
She rested her left hand on his right shoulder and peered through the window. "I have a solution."

He waited for her to finish, but when she didn't, he urged her to continue. "Well, what do you suppose I do then?"

Margaret finished her drink and said, "Rick Cleaver."

After a moment of contemplation, he turned his head and looked at his wife. Ellery took another swig and sat in silence. Margaret knew her husband was playing both sides of the line, always did. It is how she got to live the opulent lifestyle, the life she enjoyed to some degree. She would rather die than see it threatened. She drank too much when at home, however, when she was on public display she could crow with the finest of ladies. Her advice came seldom, yet it was, without fail exactly what should be done.

"I'll send him a telegram in the morning, right now I have business to take care of in town." He stood and faced his wife, put his hands on her shoulders, and kissed her on the forehead. She smelled like gin.

CHAPTER 9

Slick Jones hated going to church, but if he wanted to be sheriff one day then he would have to try and enjoy it. He was made of flesh, bone, and blood and like any man he had ambitions. He had been the deputy of Lewisburg for three years now and during that time he had killed a few rustlers, hung a few murderers, and jailed his fair share of rabble-rousers. He had proved himself. If there were any doubts about the man's ability and willingness to uphold the law, they were soon dispelled. Though he wasn't the easiest man to have a conversation with, he was polite, and the ladies found him quite charming.

Dressed in his Sunday finest he made his way to the jailhouse to let Peaty out before going to say his prayers. As he stepped into the morning light he stretched his shoulders, yawned, and donned his hat to the nearest lady, "ma'am." She nodded a polite gesture and continued along the boardwalk. The church bells tolled in the crisp morning air, which meant service would be commencing soon, so instead of setting Peaty free, he decided the drunk could wait until after he had saved his soul.

"Good morning, Mrs. Bertram."

"Good morning, Mr. Jones."

"Howdy Sam."

"Deputy."

Slick Jones was in fine spirits this morning. A night with the whore Rosa usually left him spritely. He wasn't a big man, neither tall nor short, on the slight side with shoulder-length brown hair. He had difficulty growing whiskers so he didn't get to Thompson, the barber very often, though he should have because his daughter Elsa had grown into a mighty fine woman.

Mayor Ellery was standing out in front of the church in the shade of the two big oak trees that grew on either side of the path that led to the church from the road. He was with his wife Margaret, though, unofficially, he knew the mayor quite often liaised with Sheriff Lonergan's daughter, Bernice. She sure was plump and not much to look at, but he was wise enough to know that each man has his peculiar tastes. Who was he to judge? Whenever he spoke to the mayor, he never could hide his dislike for the man. "Good morning mayor." Slick Jones donned his hat as he looked at Margaret Ellery and said, "morning ma'am, it sure is a beautiful day."

She smiled at the deputy. Mrs. Ellery had heard her husband complain about the deputy, but she found him charming. "Good morning to you Mr. Jones. It is a splendid day. I find such occasions divine."

"Yes ma'am. I can certainly understand why. Have you seen the Sheriff?"

His question was ignored.

Ellery was frustrated. He found Deputy Jones quite hard to work out. Therefore, he had decided that he didn't like him. More than once he had asked Sheriff Lonergan to fire him, but he refused. "You won't find many men as good as Slick in these parts." Despite his dislike for him he had to agree with the sheriff on this point. "I wish they'd stop ringing those damn bells."

The bells ceased and it was time to move inside the small church for service. The crowd filed in silently and Deputy. Jones was the last to walk in the church and sat closest to the exit.

The room was a hive of conversation, which started quietly at first but as it went unchecked the noise in the room got louder. When Pastor Morton entered the room, the parishioners fell silent. An instant hush settled over the room and as Slick looked around, he saw familiar faces but was surprised to see Thorn Hannon and Sarah McKinnon sitting together. Their presence piqued his interest.

Pastor Morton's voice rose as he said, "The revenger of blood himself shall slay the murderer: when he meeteth him, he shall slay him."

It was the day after Will Lonergan was gunned down in the main street, and while the townsfolk accepted that he had died from an act of violence brought about by his hand, his death had unsettled the town. Such an opportunity usually gave the Pastor a reason to sound more righteous and holy than ever before, and he made the most of it.

Slick Jones looked at the unusual couple again and wondered what they were doing together. He hoped the mayor saw them too. He took some comfort in Ellery's displeasure. The thought of it made him smile and he had to stifle some laughter.

The Pastor's voice rose even higher, "Moreover, ye shall take no satisfaction for the life of a murderer, which is guilty of death: but he shall surely be put to death."

After singing a few hymns and finishing with the Lord's Prayer the congregation dispersed. It was customary to mingle out front of the church for a time. It was a great opportunity for those who lived great distances to catch up with friends and family. As Slick Jones rolled a cigarette a firm hand clapped him on the back, and he dropped his tobacco in the dirt. He turned sharply and caught the eye of Thorn Hannon looking down on him. He eyed the man cautiously and said, "I reckon that sermon was written for you especially."

They stared at one another for a while. Both men were looking for a weakness in each other, apart from what they knew already.

Slick cut to the chase and said, "so you killed Will Lonergan?"

Thorn nodded in agreeance and said, "he had it coming. I have always known he murdered Wade. I was just waiting for the right time."

Slick was silent for a moment and considered his words wisely. "He brought it on himself, but the Sheriff isn't going to forget. I didn't care for him, but his brother did."

"Perhaps. He is a broken man Slick. I've already spoken to him."
"I heard."

Thorn scratched his head and continued, "I take it the sheriff and the mayor are pretty close."

"Why don't you ask them yourself," Slick hissed. He was at a loss as to why he was being harassed. He eyed Thorn calmly and said, "if you've got something to say, spit it out and stop jawing."

"Alright, Sarah told me about your little visit. Listen closely, listen well, McKinnon and Hannon's soil are not for sale."

Jones was offended, "I don't like your insinuation."

"What were you doing there, Deputy?"
"I was following orders."

"You seem like a smart man Slick, so I'll tell you how I see it. Ellery is no good and you need to stop following your orders and dig around some."
"What are you suggesting, Thorn?" I haven't broken the

law, Thorn. I haven't, and if you suggest one more time, I'm on the take I'll fill you full of lead."

The big man stood tall. There was a fire in the eyes of the deputy, and he watched him closely. He believed him. "That's all I wanted to know."

The deputy broke free of his grasp and said, "Mr. Hannon you've got me figured wrong."

"Mr. Hannon," Thorn turned as Ellery approached, from behind.

"Don't make a habit of sneaking up on me," he said the next words deliberate and slow, "Lloyd, I don't appreciate it."

The man riled him, but he smiled appropriately and pretended the barb didn't hurt. "I don't believe we have been formally introduced." He held out his hand, but Thorn ignored it.

Thorn looked to the deputy and back to the mayor and said, "get to it, what do you want?"

"I admire your frankness sir; you and Miss. McKinnon do not admire small talk." Now it was his turn to fire an insult back. "It must make for delightful dinner conversation."

There was a moment's silence while Ellery considered his question. "Why did Miss. McKinnon inform me to talk to you when I offered to buy her land?"

"Our land," Thorn said matter of factly. He watched the mayor's expression and laughed at the confused look in his eyes.

Ellery was annoyed at the confusion. "I was talking about Miss. McKinnon's property, not yours, I believe it belongs to her."

"Incorrect."

Ellery turned to see Miss. McKinnon behind him, she was prettier than he first gave her credit for. Although her facial features were thin and determined there was beauty and spirit in her eyes. She smiled and said, "our land."

Thorn pushed his way through the two men, put his arm around her waist, and smiled. "Haven't you heard?"

"Heard what?" Spat the mayor.

Miss McKinnon took a step towards the men and whispered, "we're getting hitched, therefore it's our land, and it's not for sale."

CHAPTER 10

Sheriff Lonergan lay in a drunken stupor on the bunk
in the unused cell of Lewisburg's jailhouse. His dreams
were heavy, and he tossed and turned all night. He lay in
the cell next to Peaty who the deputy locked up earlier in
the evening before Lonergan had over-indulged himself.
His murmurings didn't wake the town drunk, Peaty. He
was used to such a life and he slept peacefully. Lonergan
snored so heavily and slept so soundly that he didn't hear
the stranger enter the office until he rattled a tin mug
across the bars of the cell. He sat up on the bed, unsure of
where he was. His head hurt and his mouth was dry. It
took him a solid minute to regain his senses before he
staggered to his feet. Pushing past the stranger, he
stumbled outside to the horse trough and dunked his
head. After about a minute, in which the tall stranger
thought for sure the sheriff would drown, he withdrew
his head and gasped. He ran his fingers through his hair,
flicked his hands to dispel the water, wiped them down
his shirt, and made his way back up the stairs and into the
office. Silhouetted against the morning light streaming
through the door, he looked a mess. His shirt was
untucked and the star that was pinned to his chest was
askew. Water dripped down his pants, onto his books,
and wet the floor. He straightened and squinted at the
visitor and staggered across to the stove, stirred the coals,
put on some small logs, and set the coffee to boil. Once

the coffee was on, he relieved himself in what passed for a toilet in the cell, sat down, and put his feet up on the desk.

The man was tall, well over six feet, thin with a long nose that protruded over thin lips. He was a hard case and Lonergan had seen his type before. He was a drifter, caught between the wind that blew in all directions. He was the type that scoured the land looking for opportunities to make quick money. It was a high-risk trade because quick money meant dangerous work. He was of an age when a man begins to slow down, but not many men in his trade lived long enough to do so. This indicated to the lawman that the man was good at his trade or lucky. More than likely both. When he spoke, he couldn't hide the hostility in his voice. "Who am I looking at?"

The stranger didn't like what he saw. He believed the lawman was foolish and he wasn't impressed. Still, he had no other need for the lawman than to answer some questions. If he proved incapable of answering them, which he certainly appeared to be, he would find someone who could. "Brett Langford."

The sheriff wasn't in a mood to be friendly. "What can I do for you, Mr. Langford?"

He removed the tobacco from his pocket and began rolling a smoke. When he had finished rolling the sheriff held his hand out. The man handed him the cigarette. He sat in silence while he rolled another, lit it, and said, "do you reckon the coffee would be hot enough? I sure could do with one."

"Not yet."

While the coffee boiled, both men eyed one another up. They read each other's body language, the way they moved and carried themselves. It evokes a feeling in a man that lets him know where he stands. It gives him an indication of what he is up against. Ten years ago, Lonergan would have been a fair match for Langford, but not now. He was past his prime and Langford was his superior in every way. Gun and fist, it didn't matter, Langford had the lawman dead to rights. The thought angered the lawman and he couldn't bite on the silence any longer. "I said, what can I do for you? Say your piece or vamoose."
Langford was in his element. He took pleasure in riling folks. He exhaled a ring of smoke and said, "I'm looking for someone."

The sheriff leaned forward and placed both elbows on the table, his chin in his hands. "Well, you best tell me who you're looking for Mr. Langford."

Langford's eyes pierced the glare of the sheriff and at that moment Lonergan realized the stranger was not to be messed with. "Thorn Hannon!" He said the words slow and he picked up on a movement from the Sheriff that told him he knew the man.

Now he was interested. Langford was not the type of man Hannon would associate with. He could tell by the way he carried himself. They were the kind of men who would find one another at the other end of the barrel. "Before I tell you whether I know him or not, I reckon you should explain your reasons for finding this fella."

"That's none of your business, lawman."

"Sure, it is. I can't have you shooting innocent men. This is my town and my county. One step out of line Langford and I'll bust your chops and you'll end up behind bars."

"You'll try, Sheriff. And you will die. But at least you'll die trying."

"Get out."

"What?"

Lonergan had found some starch and he was having none of the man's attitude. "Leave and the next time you walk in here be a mite respectful for the law and the man you're trying to find answers from."

"Look at you, Sheriff. You have no right to talk about respect."

Lonergan had enough of the stranger's smart mouth. He stood hastily and the legs of the chair scraped across the floor. "Try me, Langford. I am in the right frame of mind and don't think you'll have it all your way. State your business or leave. It's up to you."

Langford was laughing on the inside, but he dared not show it. He held his hands before him in a sign of resignation. "I'm sorry. Sheriff." he wasn't. "I've been on my own for too long. I'll tell you why I'm looking for Hannon."
Lonergan pointed to the stove. "Coffee?"
When they had settled back down across from one another, Langford appeared to relax, but a change had come over him. He looked his age and as his brow furrowed the lawman could see the concern written all over the man's face. "He murdered my brother."

He eyed the stranger warily and took a moment to respond. "Murdered or killed?"

"It doesn't matter."

"In the eyes of the law, it matters a lot. It's the difference between hanging a man and letting him go free."

Langford shrugged. "Killed him, I guess. But that ain't the point."

"Then what is?"
He slammed his hand down on the table. The noise startled Peaty and woke him from his liquor-filled sleep.

Lonergan unlocked the cell and grabbed Peaty by the scruff of the neck. He guided him to the door and pushed him onto the porch and closed the door. As soon as he sat back down Langford continued. "You've heard all you need to know."

Lonergan smiled, swung back in his chair, and put his feet up on the table. "Mr. Langford, I suspect you and I have more in common than you think."

"Now, mister I don't quite understand."

"Langford, Thorn Hannon shot my brother right in that street."

"Sheriff, I reckon that since you wear the badge you ought to find him and tighten the noose around his neck."

"Langford, my brother, among other things, was a hothead. He started it and Hannon finished it. It's a solid case of self-defense."

The stranger said it low and straight. "But he was your brother."

"I ain't forgot, but a lot is going on around here Langford that you ain't privy to. It ain't as simple as what you're saying."

"Life is rarely ever simple."

"Tell me, where did he run into your brother? Hannon ain't wanted by the law, I know that much. So, you're on a personal mission, now, that does pique my interest."

There was a moment of silence before the tall man asked again, "so where can I find Thorn Hannon?"

"Not so fast mister, I might not turn a blind eye, especially if you don't tell me how your brother got killed." The sheriff rose and poured himself another mug of coffee. He leaned over Langford's right shoulder and filled his mug up. "Okay, Langford, you can start when you are ready."

He summoned up the nerve to tell his story, again. Every time he told it he became laden with emotion. But he figured that the sheriff would be more sympathetic to his cause. "It was in Drywater a little over a year ago. Charlie had just driven a load of beeves for Tanner over by Butter Springs. It was the end of the trail and he and the boys let their hair down and had a few drinks and a few whores. Well this one whore, rejected Charlie's advances, said he smelled bad. Imagine that, a whore telling anyone that they smelt too bad for a poke".

Lonergan just grunted.

"Well, Charlie became offended and beat the whore to death. If I recollect correctly Marshal Toch was down in Ford County trying to chase down some rustlers. Now, Thorn Hannon was his deputy at the time and as he walked into the bar Charlie shot at him and missed. The deputy lifted his rifle and shot Charlie straight through the heart."

"You say, Thorn Hannon was the deputy in Drywater?"

"Why yes, Sheriff I thought you would have known."

The sheriff looked at the man who was becoming less of a stranger and said, "your brother shouldn't have beaten the whore to death."

"Don't you think I know that? But he was my brother and I aim to see things right. I made Mama a promise which I aim to keep."

"It's not wise to make promises."

"Well, it's done, and I'll abide by it."

"Thorn Hannon, ain't no choir boy."

"I can handle myself."

"Yes, Langford, I reckon you can."

"Are you going to tell me where he is?"
A sense of duty had overcome him. "No, Langford. I can't do that. But I'll tell you what I can do."

"What's that?"

"If anything happens to Thorn Hannon, I'll come looking for you."

The man stood and glared at the lawman who warned him. "I don't take kindly to threats."

"The law is the law and I'm duty-bound to uphold it."

"What about your brother. You are honor-bound by blood to avenge his death."
"You are wrong Langford. My brother was no good. Damn it, I am no good. And any man who beats a woman to death is no good."

He raised his voice. "She was a whore."

"As I said. Any man that beats a woman to death is no good. Your brother was no good, Langford."

Grabbing the chair, he picked it up and threw it against the wall behind the sheriff. It shattered into pieces and fell to the floor. "He was your brother."

"Only by blood."
Langford turned sharply and left the lawman standing behind his desk.

CHAPTER 11

"Good morning, Henry."

Henry Reynolds, the telegraph operator, lifted his head and smiled at the mayor. "It's a good morning to you too, Mr. Ellery."

Ellery stood before the window of the telegraph office in his Sunday finest. Church had just finished, and the day was still young. He ran his fingers down his shirt and fiddled with the buttons. Lloyd Ellery didn't stop. There was no time for rest. He believed idleness was for those who found no favor with their lot in life. A man that spends his time idly is content to let life pass him by. Time may be an infinite resource, but a person's life was measured by it. He had work to do and set about the task of strengthening his position in Lewisburg. The death of Will Lonergan couldn't have been further from his mind. The mayor tapped the counter and hummed a tune that Henry couldn't put a name to. "I'd like to send a telegram, please."

The old man became animated, pleased that he was able to be of assistance. In his estimation, Ellery was the right man to change Lewisburg for the better. He considered himself a good judge of character, despite being married four times. He was an avid supporter of the mayor as he believed that you couldn't stop progress so there was no use in trying. It was like trying to stop a stampede by standing in front of the rushing cattle and expecting them to listen to you when you ask them to stop. It was forlorn and while he understood the motives of McGee and his backers, he considered them a mite foolish. Trying to keep towns from growing was as ridiculous a notion as trying to keep your children from doing the same. In the same manner, and on more than one occasion, when he was of a mind to discuss such things, he argued that resistance was futile because all things grow. Flowers take seed, bloom, wilt, and die. Dogs are born, though they are at first dependent on their mothers for sustenance, grow soon enough, age, and die. People, much the same. Life interferes with all things and some grow older, more mature, wiser. Some flowers bloom once, others all year round. In much the same way he felt that cities and towns would eventually die. But he reasoned that they would become dead in spirit. The meaning and purpose of places would be lost in the rush for progress and profit. Henry had spent some time contemplating that very issue and he understood where those who disagreed with the mayor were coming from, it is just that you couldn't stop it. No sir, the mark of progress and civilization was too strong to repel. It was as useless as trying to erase history. All people could do, was adjust as best they could. He thought the mayor was exactly what Lewisburg needed. If it wasn't Ellery it would have been some carpetbagger with a different look, but his words and his motives would have been just as cold. Before Ellery turned up, the town was dying a slow death. He didn't figure he'd live long enough to see the railroad come through town but reasoned it would be a mighty nice thing to see, all the same.

The old man stood and received the note the mayor passed, him. "Thanks, sir. "I'll get onto it right away."

"Thanks, Henry. As soon as you get a reply. Find me."

"Yes sir."

Ellery fished two dollars out of his pocket and laid them on the small counter. "That's for the telegram and the rest is for you."
The old man looked more than happy with the offering. "Thank you, Mr. Ellery.'

He turned to walk away but stopped and turned. "Henry."
"Yes sir."

 "Not a word to anyone. Not even the sheriff."
He nodded his agreement and set about the task. "As soon as it comes, I will put it in your hands myself."

"Thanks, Henry, sure do appreciate it." He turned to walk away but the telegraph operator wasn't finished with the conversation just yet. "That sure is a pretty tune mayor, say, what is the name of that ditty?"

"Can't say as I rightly recall Henry. Don't forget now, right away."

"Yes sir, you can count on me."

Ellery wasn't listening, he had other thoughts on his mind as he stepped down into the street. Circumstances had changed. On the morning he visited Sarah McKinnon and his more than reasonable offers were rejected, Will Lonergan was gunned down by Thorn Hannon. That evening the sheriff disrespected him. The sheriff's manner surprised him, but he would give him the benefit of the doubt, after all his brother had just been killed.

That morning he learned that Hannon and the feisty Miss. McKinnon were to be married. Their union displeased him. Their marriage would make them the largest landholders in the area. Therefore, they were a threat to his plans. He wanted the land, and just this once he would prefer to abide by the law and acquire the land legally. In the past, he didn't mind other people getting their hands dirty for him. It only took him a hundred dollars, which he hadn't paid, for the sheriff to ensure that Wilson had an accident. He had learned long ago that men have the same principles, it is just that for some they can be bought at a cheaper price than the rest of them.

His influence within the town was threatened. He needed to mend his relationship with the sheriff and fast. He would have to pay the man what he was owed. Then he would sweeten the deal by offering him more than twice that for another favor. He just had to work out the finer details. Of course, there was Marlowe. He had little influence over the saloon owner, but he knew Lonergan did. He shook his head in disgust. His only ally in his nefarious activities was a lawman past his prime. He had a few loose ends to tie up. Eventually, he decided that he needed more time to think, so he made his way home.

He found his wife in the upstairs room. Despite the time of day, she was tipsy. Her drink of choice, gin. He never complained. Just like she never complained about his late-night visits to town. He found his chair by the window, pulled back the curtain, and closed his eyes.

"Did you send the telegram?"
"I did."

"How long do you think it will take to hear from him?"

He didn't know the answer to the question so ignored it altogether. "I think it may be time to cut ties with Sheriff Lonergan."

She laughed and moved across to the bureau to pour herself another gin. "I warned you about him."
She did, but he wasn't in the mood for a lecture.

"Drink?"
He ignored her. She didn't take it personally. Moving across to her chair she sat leisurely and sighed. "Lloyd, if you continue on the current course of action with that good for nothing lawman, he will bring you down."

He opened his eyes and stood before the window, then moved across the room and kneeled in front of his wife. "He needs to die."

She stroked the side of his head and peered into his eyes. Often he was a child rather than a man. At another time and place, she wouldn't have even bothered to wed him. It was a marriage of convenience. It was a union formed of need, not desire. As she stared at him, she realized that that need was at its end. Ellery needed his wife because she was strong, witty, and independent. She fed the fire that burned within him. She encouraged and nurtured him, but she would cope without him. She would survive on her own. She was tired of Lewisburg. The place and the people were beneath her. The man who knelt before her with that pitiful look in his eyes disgusted her. She hid the look of disdain she suddenly felt for the man and repeated what he just said. "He needs to die." But she was thinking of a completely different man than the one her husband had in mind.

CHAPTER 12

Langford shouldered his way through the batwings of the Dusty Boot. His entrance was distracting for the other patrons and they turned to watch the big man enter and stroll towards the bar, which ran along the back wall of the room. They turned back to their muted and stilted conversations. The man behind the bar was large and unkempt. He waddled when he walked. It appeared to Langford as if the man lived in a permanent state of filth. He disliked him at once.

"Whiskey."
The barman responded without haste and sat the drink on the bar before the stranger. "Haven't seen you around before mister?"

"That's right."

"My name's Marlowe. I'm the owner of the Dusty Boot."
Langford wasn't in a sociable mood. His conversation with the Sheriff riled him. "Your sheriff is no good." Marlowe took a step back and the other patrons turned to face him.

He kept his back to them as he continued his tirade. "He's a drunk and a fool."

"Sheriff Lonergan," began Marlowe, but he was cut off.

"Lonergan is a coward."

Marlowe was smart enough to know that it wasn't in his best interests to rile the man, any more than he was. The loyalty he felt to his friend was subdued by his sense of safety. He began wiping the bar. "What makes you say that, stranger?"

He ignored the barkeep's question and sat on his thoughts. He was silent for some time. The lawman was right, his brother, Charlie, was no good. He had no right to beat a woman to death. He knew it, always had. The youngster was his mother's favorite and when news came through that he was killed in that manner she ailed significantly. He always thought it was from a broken heart. The doctor tried to tell him differently, but he wasn't having any part of the medico's gab. There are just some things doctors don't understand. They think they do, but they just don't. He was convinced of that.

He was loyal. Family mattered. Blood was thicker than water. His father had taught him as much during the formative years of his life when he took his son under his wing. He respected his father and left with him, against his mother's wishes, when the law came calling. In the ensuing shootout, one lawman was dead, and another was seriously wounded. The family's name was mud and wasn't worth two licks of a cow's tongue. The boy who escaped with the older Langford that day did so undetected. He was eighteen at the time. His brother was ten. Charlie spent his youth growing up under the tutelage and guidance of his mother. He learned differently, but much like the man who leaned against a bar in Lewisburg, he had been changed by his experiences. Why he felt the urge to beat the whore to death baffled most folks, but his brother knew the reason. It was humiliation. The Langford's had always suffered humiliation by the folks that called themselves neighbors. Being a neighbor doesn't make one neighborly. He had learned the hard way. Every time someone uttered an oath or a rumor the eldest son challenged the accuser. He was the man of the house when his father wasn't around, and that was a lot. Their ills and misfortune, dominated by poverty, were brought upon them by their father. He was no good and the older son who took up with him when he was barely a man gave their accusers some vindication of their stance. When his mother made him promise, he did so willingly. His brother may not have had the same pride in the Langford name that he did, but he would be loyal till his death. In many ways, he and his brother were completely different. The younger was more philosophical and forgiving, where he was pragmatic and relentless. His sense of right and wrong was rooted in an understanding that no matter where you went or how far family members drifted apart from one another there was always a bond that united them. Blood. He loved his mother, though she found it hard to return it. He was his father's son, in looks and mannerisms. In many regards, she had come to scorn her eldest child as much as his father. But whenever she needed anything, money, or revenge. He was there. In his estimations, his brother had been careless in that regard. Brett Langford would do anything she asked, even kill.

He drained the glass. "Another."

Marlowe moved along the bar and responded to the request.

Langford cupped the glass and resumed his thoughts.

The room fell back into rhythm and the patrons returned to what they were doing before he disturbed them.

He had ridden with his father for six years before his luck ran out. His old man was riddled with bullets by the members of a posse at a place called Willow's Bend. His father stood in front of him as bullets tore his flesh to pieces. He managed to escape, but only just. The image was strong, and the memory made him angry. His father had died for him and if need be, he would die for his mother. His sense of honor was born out of a troubled childhood. It was shaped by the man who by nature is expected to protect him. In the end, he did. It didn't matter to him where or when he met his maker, all he was concerned with was making sure that he was true to himself and the Langford name which would die with him.

Eventually, he calmed down and was ready to speak. "Barkeep."
Marlowe responded amicably to the man's gentle tone.

"Yes sir. What can I get you? Another drink? A room? Something to eat? Perhaps a woman?"

He shook his head. "Just some information."

Marlowe stood opposite Langford with the palms of his hands on the bar, slightly more than shoulder-width apart. "I'm looking for Thorn Hannon."
Marlowe raised his eyebrows and whistled softly, "Are you a friend of Lonergan's?"

"The sheriff and I will never be friends."

"I don't mean him. I'm talking about his brother, Will."

"I couldn't care less about what happened to the Sheriff's brother. I am only interested in Hannon. Do you know him or not?"

"Yes, I do."

"I haven't got time to waste. Tell me where he lives, and I'll be on my way."

Marlowe considered the man that stood before him, nodded, and said. "He owns a place a few miles out of time. I'll draw you a map."
"I'm obliged."

Marlowe fussed around behind the bar and in less than a minute had drawn a crude map and slipped it to the man across the bar, like he was passing a note behind a teacher's back in school.

Langford eyed the map, folded it, and put it in his shirt pocket. He finished his drink, hitched his belt, and turned to leave.

"Stranger."
He looked over his shoulder at the ugly looking man. He raised his head slightly, "what?"

Marlowe stared into the man's cold blue eyes and gulped. The critter standing before him was one ornery cuss. He was about to remind the man that he owed him two dollars and decided against it. "It's nothing. Nothing at all."

CHAPTER 13

Langford sat on his horse atop a hill a mile from the Hannon spread. The moment had come. He had dreamt of this moment for twelve months. On the trail, sitting by a fire and lying beneath the stars, Brett Langford had waited for this moment. He licked his lips and swallowed hard. He reached for his canteen and drank heartily. Out of a nervous habit, he removed the Colt and checked its load. Reholstering, he reached down and rifled through the saddlebag to his left and removed a pair of tan leather gloves. He fixed first the left, then the right. Opening and closing his fists, he adjusted the ends. He removed his Winchester from the scabbard by his right thigh and levered a round into the breech.

He didn't care how or when Hannon died. All that mattered was that he did. As soon as he saw Hannon, he was going to kill him. No questions asked. If that was in the main street of a town or in his woman's arms, then so be it. What mattered was that he kept his promise to his mother. He had known men who had taken a certain pride in how they killed another man. He considered such romantic notions for fools and dreamers. It had nothing to do with honor, and everything to do with their ego. Fast guns were the worst for such foolish behavior. Tommy Gun, as he called himself, was a young gunfighter who met his death in such a foolish manner. Gun took more delight in the theatre of the fight, rather than the fight itself. His antics worked well enough, but he soon met his match when Kyle Harmon shot the gunman full of lead before thinking twice. It was all about survival and a man that indulged in theatrics rather than getting down to business was a fool.

But honor, that is something he understands. Honor was a feeling and it is something a man either has or he doesn't. In some, the feeling is strong, in others not so. But a man who possesses it for what it was, knows how powerful it is. Honor has no colors. There are no words fit for speaking that can describe honor to men. For it is as individual to men as their thoughts. Honor can't be taught. It can't be learned from a book. A man decides for himself what is honorable. But even that is not quite right. Honor finds him. When life, through circumstance, has stripped a man bare of all he had and all he thought he knew, honor would be the last thing to go. Often, men force their hand and try to manipulate a moment to their advantage. Such men often ended up dead, like Tommy Gun. But when honor sets a man on a course of action, he sets himself against those who have their sense of integrity. Thorn Hannon was such a man. One of them must die. If he died, then at least he took comfort that the last man who carried the Langford name did so with his head held high.

Using his knees, he guided the mount down the slope. He held the rifle across his body while he rocked gently from side to side. The road ran straight to the gates of the ranch. As he approached, he saw a sign that simply read "Hannon's." He smiled derisively, raised the rifle, and contemplated shooting the sign full of holes, but such an act would alert the man he was after and he planned to use every advantage he could get.

The ranch was in fair condition. Large parts of the earth around the house had been tilled, but nothing was growing except weeds. The corral was large and well-constructed. The highest panels were a healthy five feet. A trace ran from the barn to the corral and through to a holding yard. An overgrown vegetable garden was the first sign that gave him cause to consider the residence. He stopped the horse and dismounted. An eerie silence settled over him and it was then he realized that there were no animals. There were no horses, cows, or chickens. He looked straight ahead. The ranch house was small in comparison to most he had seen, but the moment told him that there was no one home. The place was deserted. Still, he wasn't to be careless. He slapped the horse's rump and staying vigil he held the Winchester in his left hand and palmed the Colt.

His words were strangled and terse. "Hannon."

Nothing. There was no smoke from the chimney and the woodpile next to the door was small. He called out again. "Hannon."

Silence.

He approached the house stealthily and stood with his back to the wall. Then acting on instinct, he kicked the door and it flung inwards. Stepping inside he moved the Colt from left to right as he entered the main entrance. The room was bare. He leaned the rifle by the door and moved throughout the home. The place was deserted. There was little to no furniture left and it looked like no one had lived there for some time. Langford moved back through the rooms and searched for any valuables that were left behind. Nothing. He then gathered the leftover furniture, which included a chair, a rickety old bedside table, and a dresser with a door missing and dragged them into the main room. He went to the barn and gathered some hay by dragging his hands across the floor of the barn. Returning to the house he wedged it beneath the old furniture.

In his rummaging's, he found some paper and a pencil and leaned on the bench, and scribbled a note. He picked a knife up off the floor after he emptied the contents of the draw from the kitchen. Returning to the barn he grabbed a coal oil lamp, and with vigor marched back to the main house and dumped the contents over the hay. The man smiled. He was pleased with himself. It wasn't the first house he had burned to the ground. Rolling a smoke, he wedged the cigarette between dry lips and struck a match on his holster. After igniting the quirley he dropped the match and it fell on the oil and initiated a dull thick flame. He readjusted the hay so it would ignite quicker, picked his Winchester up by the front door, and exited the building. His mount hadn't wandered far, and he managed to sheath the Winchester and lead the mount to the barn which was two hundred yards from the main building.

He turned to face the house. Through the door, he saw the flame. He watched it grow. Its intensity increased and by the time he had finished his smoke and ground it out with the toe of his right boot, the house started to hiss and spit. Moving across to the barn door he put the piece of paper against the door and drove the knife into the weathered timber.

Langford mounted and rode out of "Hannon's'" at a leisurely pace. When he got to the sign, he removed the rifle and without aiming, shot a hole through it. He repeated this action over and over again. The report sounded at least a dozen times. The echo of each shot ringing out across the valley. The impact of each slug splintered timber and the sign fell, only to be left hanging by one piece of wire. Feeling proud of himself he rode to the top of the hill and turned the mount. The place that Hannon, at one time or another, called home was well alight.

Langford nodded slightly, pulled the reins to the right, and nudged the mount.

CHAPTER 14

Sarah had woken early and prepared to make the long ride into town. She was picking up supplies, including her wedding dress and Thorn Hannon was not invited. He was up before her, of course, to get the wagon ready and by the time he made his way inside, his breakfast was on the table, and coffee was in the pot.

Thorn said jokingly. "If the folk of Lewisburg knew we were living in sin before the big day, they would consider it a scandal I'm sure."

Sarah sat the coffee down in front of her groom to be. "On the front page of the Argus, I'd say. It'd give those old cronies something to gossip about that's for sure."

Through a mouthful of food, he said, "are you sure you don't want me to come with you?"

She shook her head "What good would you be? You'd just get in the way; besides, you can't see the wedding dress until the day, don't you know its back luck to do so."

He wasn't disappointed. Truth be told he had plenty of work to do. He wanted to ride back to his ranch and make sure everything was alright. Although they had decided to live at the McKinnon spread, he didn't want his ranch to fall into disrepair. It had been a good six months since he abandoned the place, but he figured they'd need the place one day, and keeping it free of squatters was one of his priorities. Anyway, he figured it was best to stay out of Sheriff Lonergan's way. He didn't see the need to test the man's reluctance for revenge. "I'm taking a ride out to the ranch this morning. I'll be gone all day."

"I'll make you some lunch to take with you."

He nodded and watched his fiancé fuss about the kitchen. She moved gracefully as she seemed to glide across the floor. She was a strong woman. Her limbs were long and sinewy. Sarah was strong, physically, yet free of spirit. She laughed readily and saw the positive where there was only its opposite to be seen. In contrast, he was stern and serious. He was matter of fact and only dealt with facts. It could be said that he was monotonous and in some regards that was a true statement, but there was more depth to the man than people initially thought. Sarah had seen this instantly, and though she was eight years younger, she felt an instant liking for her neighbor. Their courtship developed quickly. After three months of living alone, they became engaged. Three months after the engagement he left the Hannon spread forever. Their union was not merely a practical arrangement. They both saw in each other a part of themselves, yet there was something within that bound them together. It was hard to express, but they felt it true enough. Thorn had contemplated selling the land, but since they were financially sound, there was no rush to offload it. Perhaps he would lease it out for grazing. Memories of his childhood were strong, and he was still attached to the place. It was the resting place of his parents and his brother. It didn't feel right abandoning them. His parents were beyond decent. They were good folks. They worked hard, taught their sons well. Their message was simple. A man is responsible for his actions. He must admit to his faults and take responsibility for who he is. He is to offer no excuses. His father, who was considerably older than his mother, died of cancer. His mother died from pneumonia the following winter. He was the adventurous son and sought to understand the world and his place in it from the saddle. Most of the things he had learned, he did so from the saddle. These included the love for nature, the importance of family, beauty, and the benefits of a simple life.

Sarah filled a canvas sack and set it on the floor by his feet, before sitting opposite him. The kitchen was small and cosy. They ate in silence for a while, content to be in one another's company, and contemplate their day ahead. The incident with Will Lonergan was at the forefront of Hannon's mind. It was easy to tell yourself you shouldn't dwell on such events, but harder to heed your advice.

"Mrs. Brady likes to fuss so; I may be a while, but I'll be home before dark."

Thorn saw Sarah to the wagon, and she climbed up without his assistance. She was independent in every way and he had no desire of getting in her way and confining her duties to the household chores. She was too much of a woman to accept such a life, especially if she didn't agree with it. She slapped the reins and the mounts jerked forward. He stood in the yard and watched her depart. The day was young, and he had lots of riding to do so he made preparations for his departure.

Sarah enjoyed the peace of the journey into town. She recalled the visit from the mayor and the lawmen, two days ago. It was the first visit and she doubted it would be his last. She expected him to call on her eventually. Since Ellery had moved to town his take of the surrounding holdings didn't go unnoticed. The murder of Wade Hannon was linked to the land grab by the mayor. Of course, she couldn't prove it, but one's instinct quite often proves to be true. She was on the verge of selling when Thorn Hannon returned home. Their families were close, and they had grown up around one another. He was the last known connection she had to Lewisburg.

Considering her land was a grazing paradise due to its location beside the Canyon River, she knew Ellery would make a move on it. It made sense to her that the man in question wouldn't take rejection too kindly. She thought he was an awkward little man. It appeared to her that he expected other people to act a certain way in his presence that favored him. It that way he was pretentious and ill-conceited. In her estimations, he portrayed a misguided understanding of his self-importance. He assumed that because of his position he was entitled to a modicum of respect. He was wrong. A person just needed to be who they were, and then every man and woman would be able to judge based on their dealings with one another whether they were worthy of such pomp and ceremony. It just so happened that Ellery and his kind had grown in number, and people, in general, had an inflated presumption of their importance in the lives of others. In reality, those others couldn't care less. Their earthly trials were far removed from an egotistical upstart who considered themselves more virtuous than their counterparts. Her view of him was reinforced when she met him again after the church service. She took delight in the man's discomfort and couldn't hide the grin that appeared on her face as she rounded a bend in the road and Lewisburg came into view.

Lewisburg shimmered in the mid-morning heat. She had traveled the same way into town ever since she was a child. The saplings to her right had dispersed themselves across the land, though they had always been the same height for as long as she could remember. Quite often she rode into town with her father, who she was close to. He was a genial and easy-going man who liked the rigors of hard work and saw value in it. He believed a man without toil was less of a man. On the occasions they rode into town for supplies she would always leave with a pocket full of boiled lollies. Through labor, a person learned patience, virtue, and the value of a dollar. Her father got thrown from a bronc when she was fourteen. He lingered for a few weeks before dying from a head injury suffered in the fall. She was raised by her mother who never remarried. She was a hard woman and strict and took over the role of disciplining her daughter from her husband. In many ways, she was too hard, but both men and women needed to display a steely reserve to survive. Even though it was only a generation or two hence what was required of her to eke out a living was vastly different than what her parents were required to do. She possessed a discreet gentleness in her eyes and a fluidity of motion that the daughter inherited. Sarah admired her mother for many reasons, and if she ended up being half the woman she was, she would be content. She just didn't want to be so damn hard.

She rolled the wagon past the 'welcome to Lewisburg sign' and though it was mid-morning the town was alive with activity. She nodded her greeting as she passed and the wagon jutted gently as she came to a stop.

Two men were sitting in front of the Dusty Boot Saloon. They were Marlowe and his new friend, Langford. It was the latter who spoke. "Who's the woman?"

"That Mr. Langford, is Thorn Hannon's bride to be."

Langford had shown little interest in Marlowe even though the latter had tried hard to make conversation with him all morning. When Langford returned to the saloon this morning, Marlowe was intrigued as to the man's whereabouts and tried his hardest to find out where he had spent the night. Langford was smart enough to know that you don't spend your life answering questions, a man is better off asking them. When asked if he found Hannon he replied, "either Hannon or I would be dead. Either way, you won't see me again."

Langford watched the woman enter the haberdashery, rose, and said, "I think I'll introduce myself."

Marlowe wanted to pay the man scant regard, but he just couldn't.

"Good morning Mrs. Brady."

Mrs. Brady could see the smile on Sarah's face and couldn't help smiling as well. "I've been waiting for you, Miss. McKinnon, I have your dress right here."

She waited patiently, yet excitedly as Mrs. Brady disappeared into the back room. Sarah took the dress from her when she returned and held it against herself and looked in the mirror. A smile stretching across her face. "May I try it on now, she asked." Looking at the seamstress with anticipation.

"Of course, dear, follow me."

The ladies didn't see Brett Langford looking through the window. He said out loud, "a mighty fine lady indeed."

Sarah came out of the fitting room with the dress on and Mrs. Brady primped and preened to make sure the dress fit properly. She stopped and looked at the bride to be and said, "I do declare you have lost some weight; I am going to have to take that dress in." She rumbled around in the back for some white cotton and became flustered when she couldn't find it.

"Is everything all right Mrs. Brady?"

"I must apologize, Sarah, I seem to have misplaced the white cotton, I will just duck across to the general store. I do believe Mr. McGee will have some. He seems to have the most obscure items." In a huff, she opened the door, stepped past the stranger, and headed to the general store.

The bell that hung above the door and jingled to let Mrs. Brady know that a customer had arrived, had not worked for some time. Miss. McKinnon didn't hear the man walk in the shop as she was too busy admiring her dress in the mirror. It was only when she caught a glimpse of him in the mirror that she tried to turn to confront him, but she was too slow.

Brett Langford drew his gun, put his left hand over Sarah's mouth, and said, "scream, and I will kill you."

She stood still not knowing what to do until he holstered his gun and pawed at her dress. Sarah began struggling against the tight grip of the strange man and her dress ripped.

He grabbed her by the back of the head and kissed her. He smelt like cigarettes and whiskey. It was then he heard a voice.

"Langford, I'd stop what you are doing if you don't want to die." Just like Langford, he had managed to slip into the haberdashery without being noticed.

Langford let go of the woman who promptly slapped him hard across the fast, twice, once with each hand. He turned to see a small man with a badge on his chest, with a gun in his hand.

His smile was crooked. "You must be Slick Jones."

"That's right. It seems as if we have both done our homework."

"I don't like you."
Jones disregarded the taunt. "Unbuckle your gun belt with your left hand and let it fall to the floor. Once that's done raise your hands nice and high."
Langford made a move. "I've just listened to that good for nothing barkeep singing your praises with that Colt. I ain't going to try anything."

The gun rig clattered to the floor.
"What are you planning to do, Deputy?"
 Jones stepped to the side and waved him forward with the gun. "Move it."

"You can't lock me up for that."

Jones shook his head. "I can and I will."

"Slick I…"

"Save it for the Sheriff."

Langford tried goading the lawman. "I bet you ain't so tough with that gun in your hand?"

He ignored the taunt and spoke to the woman instead. "Sarah, I want you to stay here until I get back."

She nodded enthusiastically.

Jones walked around behind the man and picked up his rig. "Let's go."

Langford refused. "What if I refuse to move?"

"Then I'll class that as resisting arrest and I'm legally obliged to shoot you."

Langford should have just waited until the woman left town and followed her. He overestimated the law's willingness to get involved. "I won't be behind bars long. You're wasting everyone's time. Especially mine."

The deputy knocked back the hammer and said, "I know you ain't deaf."

Langford turned around to give the lady a parting glance and eyed Slick Jones coldly. Stepping through the door he brushed past Mrs. Brady.

The woman looked up confused and then cast her eyes to her customer and with an urgency went to find out exactly what was going on.

Jones urged Langford along at a steady pace. Marlowe watched from across the street as the deputy guided the newcomer to town to the jailhouse. He stepped down into the street and at first warily watched the scene unfold before him. Picking up his pace he crossed the distance needed and slowed only when he stepped through the door.

The deputy turned the key in the lock, holstered, moved across to the desk, and placed the key in the top drawer.

"What did he do, Deputy?"
"That's none of your business."
Langford called out. "You've made a mistake, lawman. When I get out of here, I have a score to settle with you."

Jones ignored him and turned to Marlowe. "Have you seen the sheriff?"

The fat man shook his head and repeated his question. "Jones, what did he do?"
Once again he ignored the man and moved across to the desk, wrote a note for the sheriff, and left it in the middle of the table. They had always communicated in such a way and it worked every time.

"Marlowe, get word to the Sheriff that I have a prisoner and he needs to get here as soon as possible."

The man nodded and waddled off.

Langford ran to the bars of the cell. His voice was angry. "Where the hell do you think you are going, Deputy?"

Jones stepped out onto the porch and closed the door behind him.

CHAPTER 15

Thorn followed the river's edge south. The thick, fertile prairie grass ran up to the water's edge. The ground was soft and the wildlife abundant. Deer ran from left to right before disappearing in the strand of timber to his left. He saw the odd jackrabbit skirting through the grass. The water changed color as he rode. He knew that the features of a watercourse influenced the color of the water that flowed through it, but he took great pleasure in witnessing its beauty. Different shades of blue and green shaded the steady flow of the river. The sun reflected off the water and changed the color again. When it caught his eye at the right moment he squinted and had to look away. He heard the water trickle over rocks and around logs. Ducks, with brown and black wings, and dark circles around their eyes were plentiful. There was a tall gray bird, with long legs and a blacktop. It stuck its long beak into the mud and came up with a worm, but instead of eating it flew away to do so in private. The worm struggled but to no avail.

He recalled childhood memories. The best time he had as a boy growing up on the ranch was in this very river. Fishing with his father and swimming with his brother were memories he knew he would never forget. He and his brother made a raft they used to cross from one bank to another, though the current was never strong enough to prevent them from swimming across if they desired. The memories seemed so far away, yet they were so personal. He took them with him wherever he went. In Texas, he lay on his bedroll after a hard day's work chasing cattle and stared at the stars. Texas was a rugged, yet wholesome place. It made a man feel like he belonged to the earth, but the memories he recalled more often were those of his youth, on this land, and by Canyon River.

The leaves on the trees had started to turn brown. The days were getting shorter and the mornings and evening cooler. It was to his chores that his mind turned. The winters were harsh, and the snows were deep. He had been spending his time chopping wood and storing it wherever there was a dry roof. Most of his toil in the last few months had been about gathering, cutting, and stacking wood for the long winter ahead. Sarah had been preserving food and making sure their stocks were adequate. A few killers would be moved to the holding pen attached to the barn. They would be well fed and cared for just in case they needed extra meat. He had left the family home as a young man and he didn't truly understand the nature of working a ranch until he returned a year before. His time was spent preparing, mending, and tending to the few cattle they had. They would sell another fifty head before winter settled and keep winter stock only. Although he grew up on a ranch, he had come to realize that he knew very little. Sarah had been a great guide in that regard as she had spent all her life under such conditions. His time as a lawman in

Drywater was a fond memory and he found the work to his liking.

He was brought out of his reminiscing by the smell of smoke. He looked straight ahead, stood in the stirrups, and shielded his eyes from the sun. Thin wafts of smoke spiraled into the air, twisted, thinned out, and disappeared. The smell was faint. He removed his rifle and urged his mount forward. His heart raced, but then he reasoned that perhaps someone, maybe a drifter, had decided to call the place home. He reached the rise a half a mile from the ranch. The view looked down on the back of the ranch and further beyond to the barn and the corral. There was no smoke wafting from the chimney. The house lay in ruins. Only a charred shell of the western and northern walls remained. The stone chimney on the eastern wall was still intact. He approached slowly and dismounted two hundred yards before the bleak structure. Smoke trailed slowly into the sky. His family home was destroyed, and his first thought was sadness, which quickly turned into anger. He patrolled the edge of the burned-out building and walked right around it. His mind raced. This was no accident. But who and why?

Moving beyond the remains he made his way to the corral and the barn. It was then he saw a piece of paper on the door. Removing the knife that held it firm, he held the paper up to the light. He read it word for word, twice, cussed and read it again. Hannon stuffed it in his pocket and kicked the barn doors open. There was no one there.

The place was deserted. He at first contemplated returning to the main house, but then remembered his brother and parent's graves. He hastily made his way before them and staggered the last twenty yards and fell to his knees. They were untouched.

Three white crosses from left to right. His father, mother, and brother. They stood out against the blackened background of his home. No, their home. Weeds grew around the base of the crosses and along the edge of the graves. The remnants of flowers held fast to the dry earth. The wind picked up and a mini dust storm spun and moved erratically before disappearing. Their graves were like the dust storm. Their graves may have been symbolic of death, but in the end, they would age and fade with time. All resemblance of the men and women who inhabited the earth would be erased. Memories only live so long because those with them must wither and die. Their markers did not capture their life as well as they deserved. They were good people. Their lives were as different as their demise, yet each was bound together by blood and in the end, fate. To a stranger, names on a cross are just that. They mean nothing. They don't tell the story of the struggles, hardships, and joys of the deceased. The crosses were inadequate to satisfy the memories. Who will speak for the dead once they have gone? Who will stand up for all that the Hannon's stood for? Thorn Hannon stood, his chest heaving. A quiet rage consumed him. He removed the note from his pocket and read it out aloud.

"It's your turn to die

I'll be waiting

There can be no refusal"

He stuffed the note back into his pocket, looked north-east across the prairie in the general direction of town. He saw the sign to the ranch and approached. It swung back and forth and when he stopped before it, he saw the damage that was done. There would be retribution for the man or men who felt the need to burn his family home to the ground. He was honor-bound to right the wrongs that had befallen him. He couldn't go to the law. As far as he knew it could have been the law that was responsible. He would ride into town and lay it all on the line and to hell with the consequences. He would kill or be killed. But there must be an accounting. Justice must be served and quite often its best delivered with white-hot lead. Mounting he returned the way he had come, but at a quicker pace and instead of memories, his mind was burning with hate.

CHAPTER 16

"Are you all right, Miss. McKinnon?"

The lady in question sat on the buckboard, she was distressed and angry. She wrapped her arms around herself beneath the blanket that Jones put around her shoulders. It took her a while to answer his question as she was lost in thought. Her attacker was strong and easily overpowered her. She considered how lucky she was that Deputy Jones intervened when he did. By a simple twist of fate, he saved her from the utmost abuse.

"I'm fine. A little shaken up, but I'll be okay."

He nodded his acceptance of her response. Sarah McKinnon wasn't one to mince words. She said she was fine, so he accepted it as gospel. "I'm glad."

Jones grabbed hold of the reins as he slapped the backs of the mounts. They responded instinctively. The wagon lurched forward, and the wheels jutted on the dry earth. He had just spoken to Sheriff Lonergan moments earlier. He was making his way down the street towards the jailhouse when Jones delivered the news. Lonergan was annoyed at the intrusion. The man smelled. He needed a shave and his attire was unkempt and not befitting of office. He also smelled liquor on the man's breath during their brief conversation. The Sheriff's demise was imminent, he just didn't want to have to be the one to hasten it along. But Lonergan must be held to account, he just didn't know how to do it. Ellery and Lonergan were allies, and any move against the sheriff would bring about his downfall, especially if Ellery got his way. He suspected Lonergan was on the take but was unable to prove it. Either way, sooner rather than later, there was bound to be violence and blood in the main street of Lewisburg. Perhaps, a conversation with McGee was needed. It appeared to be a good idea and he would contemplate such a move, but first, his priority was making sure the woman got home safe.

Jones informed the Sheriff what had happened and of his intentions to make sure Sarah McKinnon returned home. His manner was abrupt, and he couldn't hide the disappointment in his voice when he spoke. Lonergan nodded and slurred his speech. His eyes were bloodshot and his skin pale. The man was fighting a losing battle against another hangover. Beads of sweat pooled on his forehead and ran down the side of his face. Lonergan wasn't strong enough to think himself out of the mess he had gotten himself into. The death of his brother hit hard. The only family he had in the world was his daughter, Bernice. They had drifted apart, due to his ill-temper and evil ways and because of her lust and quest for wealth and fame.

Slick Jones was uncomplicated. He saw things as they were and went about life accordingly. He had no favor for pomp and ceremony, but understood the importance of such frivolities, for some people. He could do without such charades. He liked his job and reasoned that the law was reasonable, though he found people to be unreasonable. Not all people of course, but there was a certain breed that made his job harder than it needed to be. He figured that it wasn't hard to be law-abiding, it's just that lots of folks preferred not to be. When the occasion arrived in which he was required to enforce the law, he was more than capable of doing so. He had commanded begrudging respect during his tenure as Deputy and had won favor on numerous occasions. The town folks liked him more than the Sheriff. He was more approachable and willing to lend an ear to a weary voice. Folks, regardless of their position, liked someone they could talk to without being judged. He possessed both charm and charisma. But sitting on the buckboard next to Miss. McKinnon, he had nothing. He didn't know what to say. There seemed to be no words, so he sat in silence and waited.

The fond memories she had of her father moments earlier when she rode into town were a distant memory. Why? All she wanted to know was, why? She had never met the man before in her life. Why did he feel he had a right to force himself upon her, and so brazenly?

The events that had surrounded her and her fiancé in the last few days were enough for a lifetime. She was more a recluse than a social butterfly. That is one of the traits that attracted the couple to one another. All she wanted to do was to go home. Then she would figure it all out. Her thoughts swiftly turned to Thorn. He would want revenge and would seek restitution for her honor. It didn't matter what she said or how much she pleaded. He would seek atonement and achieve it or die in the process. It was the type of man he was. He spoke little but when he did, he meant what he said. He followed through on his decisions. Even though the man sitting next to her locked up the abuser, Thorn would ride into town to mete out his brand of justice. It didn't matter what Jones, Lonergan or the law did, Thorn would be honor-bound, to bring the man called Langford to the task. She became concerned at the notion because the man in jail didn't appear to be the type to run away. They would clash and for one of them, it would end disastrously.

Her words were strangled and laced with emotion. "Who was he?"

Jones was contemplating little. He accepted the silence and was content with it. "His name is Brett Langford."

"I've never seen him before."

"He's not from around here. He rode into town yesterday."

"What do you know about him?"

"I know he's looking for Thorn."
Her mouth fell open and she turned to face the deputy, who kept his eyes straight ahead. The words hit her in the

chest. It took her some time to absorb what the lawman said. She had so many questions she didn't know where to begin.

"Why would this man be looking for Thorn?"
"Revenge."
"You mean?" She left the sentence unfinished.

"That's right. Langford aims to kill him?"
Her voice was desperate. "But why?"

"He says Thorn killed his brother. I believe he knew who you were and aimed to get to Thorn through you."

Sarah fell into a lull. It appeared as if she wasn't destined to have a future with Thorn Hannon. Langford's attack was orchestrated to rile the man she was to marry. "What do you plan to do?"

"I'll keep him locked up as long as I can, but I can't give you any guarantees."

The rest of the trip passed quickly enough with little more chatter and when he brought the wagon to a stop by the well in the front yard, fifty yards from the house she spoke.

"Thanks, Deputy."
Looking around the ranch he noticed it was empty.
"Where's Thorn?"
They alighted from the wagon and moved towards the house. She went to speak, and they heard an approaching horse. The rider was Thorn and he was riding fast. The

rider brought his mount to a halt as he pulled high and tight on the reins.

Thorn Hannon stared at them. His nose rose slightly, and the corners of his mouth lifted into a snarl. His brows were dark and hooded. The lines around his eyes bunched together. The latter was filled with anguish and revenge. He looked at the lawman and his fiancé and knew something was wrong.

"What the hell's going on here?"

CHAPTER 17

Deputy Jones leaned against the well smoking a cigarette. The sun started to wane, and a cool breeze felt its way off the river behind him. The death of Will Lonergan set a series of events in place that he believed would fold in on one another. Though the events weren't all related to the death of the lawman's brother, it was the catalyst that set them in motion. Life was coming to an end for some, yet though their deaths would be brief they were a long time in the making. Langford wouldn't stop until he avenged the death of his brother. The Hannon spread had also been burned to ashes. Thorn took the time to inform him of such after he dismounted, moments earlier and before Sarah ushered him inside to inform him what happened in town earlier that day. Ellery would continue to use the Sheriff, and his daughter, to his advantage and his interests. He cursed himself. It was time he did some digging around instead of being content to follow orders. It was time he addressed the private meetings between the mayor and the sheriff. He needed to investigate some of the mayor's business dealings. He was not going to be implicated in whatever Lonergan and Ellery were working on. Ignorance was not an excuse, but he allowed it to dominate his relations with the men in question. It was on such thoughts he was ruminating on when the door of the house opened, and Thorn Hannon stepped into the fading light.

Thorn approached him, carefully, "Deputy."

He turned around to face the big man, who stepped with a determined stride. His mood was somber. He seemed older than he was, and age showed in the lines of his face. He appeared somehow withdrawn and tired. Thorn held out his hand and the men shook hands.

"I sure would like to thank you."

"It was the right thing to do. Is she alright?"

His voice was hoarse, full of emotion. "She'll be fine. Sarah is a strong woman. She is more shocked than afraid. Who was the man that laid his hands on her?"

The deputy flicked his cigarette on the bare earth, "Brett Langford."

Thorn threw his arms in the air. "Seems I know the name; I just can't recollect."

Jones recalled the brief conversation he had with the Sheriff the night before. "You killed his brother for beating a whore to death, I think his name was".......

Thorn finished the sentence, "Charlie."

"That's right, so now he's aiming to kill you."

He reached into his pocket and handed the note to the lawman. "I found this on the barn door."

He read the note and handed it back, "what do you aim to do?"

"I reckon the man who wrote this note is the same man that attacked Sarah."

"I'd say you are correct."
"Then what are you going to do about it?"
"I locked the man up, but I don't know how long I can hold him. But I have no proof he's the man who burned down your place."
"Damn it, Jones, you know as well as I that it's the same man."
"I do, but I have no proof, Thorn."
"Well, it looks like I'll have to pay this man a visit."

"I figured you would and I ain't going to waste my time trying to talk you out of it, but if you break the law Thorn, I'll arrest you."

"Is that a threat?"
He shook his head. "No. I'm just telling you as I see it; how it has to be."
Thorn was exasperated and ran his fingers through his hair. "What about Lonergan?"

It was a difficult question to answer, but it was one he had already considered. "It took me a while to see it myself. I guess I just didn't want to believe the man had it in him to turn sour."

"He only keeps you around in case there's trouble. It is because of your gun, that he keeps you on as a Deputy. Sarah and I figured that out the day you rode out here with him."

"I'm beginning to believe you are right."

"You're not the same as Lonergan and you're nothing like Ellery. They are dirty, Slick. They're up to no good. I don't trust either of them. Watch your back."

Slick straightened and there was pride in his voice. "I haven't broken the law. I'm not sure about the Sheriff, but I have no evidence to convince me he has either."

Thorn nodded. He sensed a common spirit in the Deputy and understood the difficulty of his position.

"One thing is certain; the Sheriff and Langford have something in common."

The rancher nodded in agreeance, "yep, Deputy, I reckon they do."

Sarah came out of the house and approached the deputy. She was composed and steady. She looked at him intensely, as if she were trying to read the man through his eyes. Eventually, she embraced the lawman. "Thank you, Slick."

Slick began to feel uncomfortable and embarrassed, so he put his hat on. "It's time to get going."

"Your welcome to stay the night," offered Thorn.

"That's mighty fine of you to offer, but I got some thinking to do, and I do it best when I'm riding."

He unhitched his mount from the back of the wagon, mounted and without another word, beat a hasty retreat.

Both Sarah and Thorn watched him ride away in silence. Darkness slowly enveloped him, and he disappeared in the distance before they turned to face one another. They were both thinking the same thing. Who the hell is Slick Jones?

Hannon put his arm around her waist, and she laid her head on his shoulder and they walked up the stairs and through the door, which was closed gently behind them.

The deputy rode in silence. He didn't know how the Sheriff was going to respond. Well, he didn't like the Sheriff's tone when he tried to explain to him what had happened. He wasn't going to stand idle and let a lady be assaulted. It was not right and no amount of arguing could make him see otherwise.

The moon had reached its peak by the time Slick made it back to town. He didn't go to the office. An idea occurred to him while penning his thoughts to a blank sky. He needed to see Doc Henson. He had a question and it couldn't wait until morning.

CHAPTER 18

Doc Henson lived on the northern side of Lewisburg, a quarter mile past the city limits. He had an office in town and unless needed he preferred to spend his time alone. He wasn't the only doctor in town with his competitor being Doctor Dubois, but he was the oldest one and the townsfolk had come to like him, despite his eccentricities.

His house was modest but well-constructed. Its interior was sparsely furnished and untidy. Despite his position, he refused to socialize with the local dignitaries. He was too cantankerous to offer much in the way of polite conversation. As a result, he had fallen out of favor with the local elites when Dubois came to town six years earlier. Henson had no time and place for pretences. He had seen too much pain, suffering, and death in all classes of people to believe that their lives were so far removed from one another. In the end, sickness, disease, and death triumphed. He was fighting a losing battle against the ravages of stupidity and of age brought on by the relentless surge of time.

He had turned to liquor to erase the thoughts that plagued him. But he soon learned there was no remedy for the curse of mankind. The images that the liquor erased soon came back to haunt him. He found himself drinking more and more as time passed by. At first, he drank alone, and only when the work was complete. As time eluded him, the urge to drink became more frequent and he soon found himself drinking morning, noon, and night. Liquor controlled every aspect of his life and as a result, he ended up looking like a fool. He would rather stay at home and fool himself. People had been telling him for years that he was drinking too much, but it was only when he noticed it himself that he paused for a moment to consider its impact upon him. In the end, he shrugged his shoulders and persisted. He was too old to change his habits and too ornery to care. However, he still managed to retain a lot of clients. These were predominantly those who couldn't or had little means to pay for his service. He was an insomniac. This was due to his diagnosis, a combination of his work hours, and the alcohol.

The lamp was on when Deputy Jones knocked on the back door of his house at two o'clock in the morning. At first, there was no response, so Jones rapped louder.

"Alright, alright, you'll wake the bloody dead if you keep going."

Jones waited impatiently, looking from side to side in anticipation of being seen. He heard shuffling steps moving hastily across the floor. Henson answered the door and the light from the lamp on the desk behind him presented him as a clean and tidy elderly gentleman. A second glance would have concurred that the first assumption was indeed incorrect. He had a grey mustache that needed trimming and glasses that perched on a hooked nose beneath bushy eyebrows. Though his hair was unkempt he had a healthy spread of it with no signs of balding. Altogether, he didn't look like a drunk, unlike Peaty who was probably asleep under the saloon stairs again. But who knows what a drunk looks like? People were efficient at hiding their undesirable habits from one another.

The doctor had a stern character. He took off his glasses, breathed on them, and tried to clean them with the tails of his shirt, however, he ended up smudging them more than they already were. "Who are you and what do you want?"

"It's Deputy Jones and I come bearing gifts."

He eyed the man warily and then he saw the bottles in his hands, smiled and wiped his hands down his shirt, "come in, come in."

Doc Henson closed the door, which squeaked considerably, and showed the deputy to a chair near his desk, all the while eyeing the bottles of Irish whiskey the visitor was holding. "Well, what do you have there, Mr. Jones?"

Doc reached out for them and licked his lips in anticipation only to pout like a lost boy when the deputy said, "Doc, I think you know what I have and they are yours if you answer a few questions."

He took a seat opposite the visitor and leaned back, his eyes squinted as he peered at the lawman, "questions, why would a young fella like yourself have questions for me? I've got nothing to say about nothing." He wiped his hands on his shirt. He stood and then sat back in his chair, raised his eyebrows, and wiped his mouth, and gulped, trying to stave off the sweet taste of the Irish whiskey.

"One question Doc, can you do it? One question and the whiskey is yours."

"Depends on the question," he said wisely.

Jones paused, put the bottles before him on the floor, rolled a smoke, and said, "how did Wilson die?"

Doc jumped off his chair and started walking around in circles, he did this for a few minutes before returning to sit. He shuffled his chair closer to the inquirer and whispered, "I can't answer that question, Deputy."

His manner was friendly and welcoming. "Why not, Doc?"

He looked from right to left and over his shoulder. "Cause the sheriff told me not to, that's why."

"But, I'm the Deputy Doc, I have a right to know."

"Not according to the sheriff, he says you're not to know."

The lawman corked a bottle and took a swig. "It's a smooth drop, Doc."

"The Sheriff said he'd kill me if I told."

The deputy leaned forward in the chair and waited for the Doc to focus on him and said, "told what, Doc?"

"I can't tell you, deputy, I'll die for sure."

"I won't let anything happen to you."

Henson decided that it didn't matter anyway. He was dying. He had been doctoring enough to know that his time was ending. Did it matter if he died in his sleep or was killed by a corrupt Sheriff? Perhaps he'd be lying there a week or more before anyone found him. It would be a ghastly scene and one he wouldn't wish on anyone. He decided that he would risk the wrath of the Sheriff and tell the youngster what he wanted to know. Before he could formulate the right words, the lawman persisted.

"Your conscience must be eating you alive."

He laughed. "I have worse secrets. Why death ain't nothing to me. I've seen all types of deaths, Deputy. I've seen peaceful deaths and ones so painful that the only remedy for the pain was a bullet. I've seen men drop dead and some linger for years. It doesn't matter whether you are rich or poor. The color of your skin, nor your wealth will protect you from death. It will determine how you are remembered, but I guess that's what all it comes down to. In my experience Deputy, the contented man is the one who doesn't mind dying."

"Is that right?"

"Now I know you think I'm just a drunk, but you're only half right. I'm a drunk, but that's not all I am, Deputy, I'm content."

The two men looked at each other for a moment and then taking his leave from the deputy, the doctor once again wiped his hands on his shirtfront, leaned forward, grabbed a bottle of Irish whiskey off the floor, corked it, took a swig and said, "Wilson suffered from backache."

"That's good Doc, but I want to know how he died. I have a feeling he didn't burn to death."

Doc Henson repeated his previous phrase, "Wilson suffered from backache."

Deputy Slick Jones was losing hope, just as he was about to ask the question for the third time, Doc interrupted him and said, "from two slugs to the spine."

Both men sat in silence, sipping Lloyd Ellery's grand ole Irish Whiskey.

CHAPTER 19

A mild frost covered the hard ground and a chilly breeze blew in from the west. The cool water of Canyon River, miles to the west added to the crispness of the wind as it sought refuge in the streets of Lewisburg. The sun was slow to rise and the citizens of the town, caught between tradition and progress, sought the comfort of a warm fire in the morning before venturing out into the elements to leave their mark on the land.

Sheriff Lonergan, who owned a two-room house on the southern edge of town, spent most nights sleeping in the cell. Sometimes out of convenience and sometimes, because his daughter entertained the mayor, though last night was different. He had got into an argument with his daughter. She wasn't a particularly caring child, but then again, his parenting skills were quite lacking. She accused him of sloth, the sin she was rather adept at herself. But it was only the faults in others his daughter was concerned with. This resulted in him drinking more than he should have and passing out on the floor, which meant her rendezvous with Mr. Ellery was postponed. Bernice wasn't an overly nice woman, much like her mother, of which she was an exact replica. Bernice was moody and demanding. She gave no quarter and it was to be her way and to her liking. She did not consider the fact that she wanted for nothing and it was her father's wages that kept her in comfort. Her mother abandoned her father years earlier. There was no reason that she knew of. The woman simply packed her bags and left. It was often the best way to end a union such as marriage, but the departure left the lawman and his daughter with lots of questions.

Bernice was young enough to have an ideal view of the world and she most certainly possessed a naive view of men and the promises they made. She was inexperienced in such dealings and her belief that Ellery was going to divorce his wife and marry her, held. Her motivation was love, though it was more of an infatuation. It didn't matter if they hadn't been seen in public together or he had refused to put a time on when he would enact the divorce upon his poor undeserving wife. It was all too romantic to take too seriously. It was upon this very topic that her father, slightly intoxicated from the night before, felt it was his duty to impart his worldly wisdom. The timing was so important when bringing up a sensitive topic with a loved one, but then again there are times when a matter of fact and blunt approach is needed. Lonergan chose the second option. All he wanted to do was recover from his hangover in quiet. Despite this desire, Bernice felt it her duty to lecture her father, again. As soon as he opened his eyes, she began. He ignored her for as long as he could before he couldn't hold his tongue any longer. His insults were harsh but accurate. There is no point in speaking your mind without expecting others to have the same right.

She took offense to his remarks about herself and the mayor and threw a pan at him which hit him between the shoulder blades and clattered to the floor.

"He won't leave his wife for you and you're a fool if you think otherwise."
She screamed with her hands on her hips. "I hate you, get out, and don't ever come back."
He staggered slightly as he stood. Hiccupped and smiled. It was a slovenly representation of a man who had gone wrong. If he could only see himself in the mirror, then he may have cause to reconsider the path he was on, but he was smart enough not to do so. His speech was slurred, but non-committed. "It's my house."

Bernice moved hastily. She stomped when she walked. Light and delicate she was not. Standing before her father she continued her tirade. "You call yourself a father, you're barely a man. I won't tolerate you drinking in my home."

He turned to walk away but she wasn't finished yet. Walking around him, she blocked his exit and continued. "I don't want you coming home tonight. I'm not in the mood for your drunkenness. You stink. You need to bath, shave, and change out of those rotten clothes."
He tried once again to walk away, but she grabbed him by the shoulder and spun him around. "You are pathetic."

While she persisted, he watched her facial expressions. Though her features were mature she contained many of the traits of her youth. In many ways, she was still ignorant of the ways of the world and the people that made the world function the way it did. He felt a tinge of sadness because his daughter was heading for a fall and she didn't even know it. It was a moment of sentimentality that possessed him, but a moment was all it was. Her voice reminded him where he was and what was happening. He staggered to the door. The nagging persisting. Opening the door, he stepped into the morning and she slammed the door closed behind him.

He tripped and fell as he descended the stairs and quickly righted himself and looked around nervously. He was in a bad state and his daughter was right, but he was beyond caring. He didn't care about his brother, who he considered in his drunkenness the night before, a leech and good for nothing. He had no time for the mayor, who still owed him a hundred dollars. Thorn Hannon and Sarah McKinnon could go to hell. Brett Langford could suffer. That's why he left him in jail overnight, despite the man's pleading.

Things were about to change. By the time Sheriff Lonergan walked from his house to the jail he had cursed just about every man and woman he could think of., all that is, except his daughter Bernice, despite her failings, which he admitted were his own. He loved her so much.

CHAPTER 20

Mr. and Mrs. Lloyd Ellery sat at the dining table in their spacious kitchen on the bottom floor of their home. The sun shone through the wide windows and fell across the floor shattering light across the polished surface. The table was rectangular and too big for two people to sit and engage in conversation intimately. Sitting at either end of the table the couple were absorbed in their meanderings.

Lloyd Ellery was reading a week-old edition of the Argus, the local newspaper. He wanted to know what was going on in town. Quite often he would take the information from the Argus and use it to his advantage in some way. His lips moved as he read, though no sound emanated from his mouth. He also moved his head from side to side while he read. It was an elaborate display for such a menial chore. That was the man's way. In public, he was a bold character, but in private he was weak and insecure. He depended on his wife; he just didn't realize how much.

Ellery lifted his head from the Argus and looked out the window briefly before covering his face with the paper again. "Looks like rain."
His wife didn't respond, though she considered that of all the things they could have discussed before breakfast, the weather seemed so far away. It wasn't worth her time. It

was trivial and as she had begun to think, much like the man sitting across from her.

A young plump girl, by the name of Maude, walked into the room with their breakfast on a large silver tray and placed it in the middle of the table. She exited the room only to return a short time later with the required cutlery and began fussing about preparing their tea. Maude was a local girl. She wasn't too bright and couldn't read and write. She was slow to respond, but it's just the type of service they demanded. She cleaned and cooked and kept an orderly house. As long as Mrs. Ellery didn't have to work then she was content.

He coughed slightly, folded the newspaper, and lay it on the table.

She watched him fuss about his breakfast in the same manner that he did every morning. His movements were fluid and matter of fact. She considered him an unattractive man, with little to no physical prowess. She had married him to get away from her father who was impossible to live with. Now, as she sat across the table from the man she vowed to love 'till death do us part' she felt contempt.

He possessed many annoying traits that irked her. Margaret had begun to despise lots of things about her husband. The first was being brought to this god-forsaken part of the world. She played the part well and encouraged him in his business endeavors, but it was the man himself. His whinging, whining, and his frail attempts at affection had worn thin.

"Would you like a cup of tea dear?"

He nodded and smiled with a mouthful of food. He was a messy eater. As she made the tea, she put more sugar in it then he would have liked. She considered it a small victory. She stood and placed the tea in front of him, stooped, and kissed the top on his head. Returning to her seat she was satisfied that she finally committed herself to a course of action, that would change her life forever.

She was his confidant and knew almost every crooked deal the man was involved in. As far as she was concerned, he had erred when he had thrown in with the Sheriff and it was to that topic she spoke of. "Have you worked out what you are going to do with that lawman yet?"

He sipped from the teacup and his face cringed a little at the sweetness of it and it made her smile. It made her feel good.

There were two places the Ellery's discussed business and they did so twice a day, without fail. The first was at the breakfast table and the other was in the upstairs room of an evening. But this morning Ellery had been avoiding such discussion. He didn't want to face the reality that something would have to be done to silence Lonergan. Sure, he knew it must be done, but he didn't want him to die in mysterious circumstances. That would leave too many unanswered questions, and Slick Jones in charge. If Lonergan lived, then he was a liability. He considered his wife's suggestion of killing the lawman and starting afresh. He didn't like the thought of re-establishing himself in the area and wisely suggested that such a move could prove disastrous because of his relationship with Sheriff Lonergan. Maybe he could urge the Sheriff into action against Thorn Hannon. It was on such thoughts he pondered when there was a sharp and hurried knock on the front door.

The Ellery's heard the sure-footed plod of Maude and the door open. He recognized the antique voice of Henry the telegraph operator and called out. "Let him in."

The hurried yet light steps of Henry made their presence known. He stepped into the room and Mrs. Ellery smiled thinly and nodded.

The old man was breathing heavily. It was obvious he traveled quickly to bring the mayor the news. "Here's the message you were waiting for Mr. Mayor."
He took it without a word, unfolded it hastily, and read.

At the other end of the table, Mrs. Ellery watched his lips move and his head move dashingly from side to side. Oh, how she hated him.

Folding the note, he put it in his pocket and fished out a dollar note for the old man and handed it to him. The transaction happened without a word between the men.

The old man appreciated the money, but he figured that the mayor could have at least spoken a kind word to him. When he realized none were coming, he turned slowly, looking over his shoulder at the mayor and exited the room dejectedly. It was only when the door opened and closed again that his wife spoke.

"Is that from Cleaver?"

He nodded, wiped his mouth on a napkin, and stood. Moving to the end of the table he kissed his wife on the forehead again. "There was too much sugar in that tea."

He walked off and left her alone. The front door opened and closed quickly.

Margaret Ellery moved across to the cupboard, removed a small bottle of gin, and added some to her cup of tea for taste. Grabbing the cup, she moved through the hallway, opened the front door, and stepped out onto the wide porch. The sun was inviting on her face and her skin warmed gently. She moved to the railing and cast her eyes down the street. She could see her husband in his navy-blue suit. His quick stride and his arms flailing endlessly as he walked. It was a marriage of convenience followed by the mundane chores of a sedentary life. It stilted her imagination. It stifled her creativity and left her wanting more. It was an unfulfilled life, hence the gin. Her days were long and her nights too short. She was a passionate woman and longed for color and life to flower her world, but all she got instead was flour, dust, and a husband who would turn and run at the first sign of conflict. She had let life pass her by and she allowed this to happen by being content and idle. At that moment she made up her mind that she would tell her husband that she was heading home to Boston and she was doing so alone. He wouldn't cope, but she was beyond caring. Margaret Ellery had spent twenty years married to a man she did not love. Indeed, she had no affection for him whatsoever. He repulsed her and she had had enough. She would no longer play the role of the dutiful and loyal wife. As she watched him walk, she dropped the teacup into the garden and it shattered on a rock. She turned haughtily and marched through the door and slammed it shut.

She raised her voice anxiously. "Maude. Maude."

The girl was always quick to appear. "Yes, Mrs. Ellery."

"Have you ever been to Boston?"

"No ma'am. I've never left Lewisburg."

"Would you like to?"
She smiled naturally, and it caused Mrs. Ellery to smile in turn. "Why, yes ma'am."
"Excellent, now that's settled, follow me."
Mrs. Ellery bounded up the stairs with Maude at her heels.

CHAPTER 21

Lonergan opened the door of the office and moved across to the desk to get the keys to the cells. He unlocked Langford's cell, but the big man still lay on his bunk. His eyes were closed, though he wasn't asleep. The jailhouse consisted of two cells, which hardly had occupants, so Langford's stay, though unexpected, was swift.

A wood stove sat in the corner behind the door. He was setting life to the coals when Brett Langford roused. He yawned, stood, and stretched. "I take it, I'm free to go."
Lonergan blew into his hands and rubbed them in the hope he would warm himself. "No charge has been claimed against you. I've held you long enough."

He approached the badge toter. "Any sign of the Deputy. I'd like to have a word with him."
Lonergan spoke more like a desperate man searching for some lasting shreds of dignity and authority, rather than a sense of duty and loyalty. "You can do what you damn well like. But if you lay a hand on him, I'll lock you up myself."

Langford nodded. He wouldn't try to settle the score with the deputy until after he had accounted for Hannon. Still, he couldn't resist a parting shot. "That may be so Sheriff, but I've got a score to settle with him.

"I'm sure he'll be happy to oblige, Langford. But you won't outshoot him. No sir and if you lay a hand on him, well, I meant what I said."

Langford let it drop for now. "Mind if I have some coffee when it's done?"

Lonergan stood and turned his back to the stove. "Not at all. It ain't like Slick to let the fire go out."
The mention of the man's name riled Langford. "Where is he?"

The sheriff's voice was angry. "Last I saw of him he was heading south with Thorn Hannon's whore."

"Perhaps, I'll find where she lives, kill Hannon, and finish what I started."
The sheriff's laughter was mocking. "You talk big, Langford, but talking doesn't mean squat. We'll see how big you are when Hannon comes looking for you."

"I can handle my own. You'll find out soon enough, Sheriff."

"You had no right to touch her. What were you thinking?"

He moved across to the stove as the lawman simultaneously walked to his desk. As he checked the temperature of the coffee he said, "I don't like waiting around. I thought I'd force his hand. Bring him out of the cold."

"If you're so damn fired to kill him, then why don't you go looking for him?"

It had only been twelve months, but the long days in the saddle and the lonely cold nights on the trail made it feel like ten years. The sheriff would not understand. Nor did he care to explain. He had felt his way through life, and it had worked out well for him and he saw no reason to stop now. It would come to an end one day, but he had no desire to live a civilized life. Whatever that meant. He made his first two moves. The burning of the ranch was the first and his abuse of the wanted man's fiancé the second. He preferred checkers over chess, but he knew that when he and Hannon clashed it would be checkmate for one of them. "As you said, Sheriff, he'll come looking, and when he does I'll be ready."

"I'll admit," the sheriff stifled a yawn as he continued, "it was a good plan, but that doesn't make it right."

"You're a hard man to figure, Sheriff. The same man that killed my brother, killed yours. You act as if you want revenge back you are too yellow to take care of matters yourself."

"What kind of talk is that?"

"You get the meaning."

Lonergan moved across to the stove and poured himself a coffee. Langford moved across to the wall behind the desk to retrieve his gun off the hook placed there by the deputy the day before.

The sheriff turned to face Langford, eyed him coldly, and repeated his earlier taunt, "as I said, you talk big, but we'll soon see how tough you are when Hannon comes looking for you."

Langford snarled and ignored the jibe. His mind drifted to the deputy. "What about Jones?"

"What about him?"

"I figure he's going to be a mite upset when he finds out you've set me free. I don't need a rogue lawman on my tail."
"You may have to worry about him, but not yet. You should be more concerned with Thorn."

"I've summed him up, Sheriff."

"Who?"
"The deputy."

Lonergan laughed, "it doesn't pay to sum a man up son, he'll always have a way of surprising you."

The door opened and both men turned and stepped away from the door as Slick Jones entered. Lonergan moved back to his desk, while Langford stood in the middle of the room staring at him with his arms by his side.

When Jones saw the abuser, he only had one question. The question was for the sheriff, but he didn't take his eyes off the man in the middle of the room. "What's he doing out?"

"There's been no charge brought against the man. I held him for as long as I'm legally obliged."
"But I saw the man."
"According to Langford, they were locked in an amorous embrace."

"That's a lie, Sheriff."
He shrugged his shoulders. "Maybe. But no charge had been brought against him and I'm bound to let him go."
It was Langford who spoke next. "Where have you been, Slick?"

"I made sure Miss. McKinnon got home last night."

"Is that so?"
"That's right, she was mite upset after you pawed her the way you did."

Lonergan interjected. "Jones, there's no evidence to the contrary."

"But?"

"I said, we can't hold him unless a charge has been brought against him. You know that as well as I do."

Langford laughed. He took delight in goading the deputy. "I figure you can't get a woman of your own. Is that why you escorted her home?"

Lonergan had tired of their presence, besides his hangover was still there, in the background and the talking had made him conscious of it. "If you were in Langford's shoes, what would you have done?"

Jones considered the sheriff. His demeanor irked him. Much like Langford, it appeared to him that the lawman was levering the stranger to town to do his bidding for him. He was hiding behind the badge, a wave of white-hot anger consumed him. The very question was designed to test his loyalty. He was put on the spot. Still, he would play a card and see whether they upped the ante or folded altogether. "Well, I don't reckon you poke a bear while he's sleeping," the next word was designed to insult, "Sheriff," but it went over the man's head, "and wait till it runs at you."

Langford chimed in. "Then what would you do choirboy?"

The sheriff took off his hat and wiped his brow while Slick continued. "You just make sure that the bear doesn't wake up." There was a long pause before he added, "like Wilson."

Lonergan lifted his head sharply and eyed him in cold surprise. Before he could gather his thoughts, Langford, unaware of what had just taken place interjected. "You had no right to draw on me."

He poured himself some coffee and played the scene out till the end. "Well, I don't take kindly to men, who call themselves so, harassing women."

"Why don't I show you what type of man I am, sonny?"

As he made a motion towards him, Slick shifted his coffee mug from his right to his left hand. "You'll not step a yard before you die from lead poisoning. I don't recommend it."

The man paused and puffed out his chest, though it quickly deflated. Langford was many things, but a fast gun he was not. A man with an ego was a dangerous animal. Langford had a big enough ego for three men.

"What's done is done," spouted the sheriff. "I bet you a month's pay that Thorn Hannon is on his way here right now to reclaim his girl's dignity."

It was to the sheriff that Jones focused his attention. "That badge has become too heavy for you. You have no right to wear it. Don't you think it's time to move on and do whatever you plan to without hiding behind the law."

Lonergan had repeatedly denied taking Deputy Jones's badge away. He liked him, he was reliable and slippery with the gun. He needed him he told the mayor time and time again, but something the deputy said caught him off guard and ate away at him. He couldn't get those two words out of his mind. "Like Wilson," Slick had said, "like Wilson."

The sheriff stood and pushed past Langford and stopped three yards before the deputy.

"I don't appreciate the insinuation, Jones."

"You've listened to yourself too many times, Sheriff. You're a fool."

"You've got a choice to make."
The deputy shook his head in disgust. "I won't be the man you want me to be."

"Then it's settled."

Jones unpinned the badge with his left hand and weighed it carefully. His dream of ever becoming sheriff was gone. Without the badge he had nothing. That's how much it meant to him. He couldn't work for a man he didn't trust. "There will come a time," he thought twice and decided he would never call the man sheriff again, he continued "Lonergan, when you will fall. You see, I know too damn much."

Lonergan went for his gun and Langford stepped forward but the blistering speed of Jones made them both ease the reins on their emotions. Jones smiled and continued, backed towards the door with his Colt trained on the men. He found the doorknob, opened the door, and smiled. "You," he waved the barrel at the lawman, "Ellery and this critter who calls himself a man, will meet your destiny at the point of a gun. It will be a welcome justice and the citizens of Lewisburg won't mourn your death. You'd find out how much respect they had for you at your funeral, but you won't be around. I'll get a message to you, I'll find a way. But you'll know how much the people of town despise you, not for the man you were, but for the man you have become. You know me too well Lonergan and in case you have forgotten let me remind you. I'm honor-bound to make sure justice is meted out. Badge or not, I will find a way to bring you to your knees. Life as you know it is over. I'll be there when you break, and you will break. You've upped the ante, but it's your final hand, and it's a bluff."

Lonergan became enraged. "You know nothing."

Jones persisted, "and your partner, Ellery, he'll fold on you and leave you to play a lone hand. There is no pride in defeat, just regrets and you will have plenty of them."

He turned his attention to Langford. "I know you burned down Hannon's ranch. I can't prove it, but I know. Hannon is on his way into town, he doesn't carry a gun, but he'll meet you fair and square, with your fists, if you have a mind to. He's no alley cat. He won't shy away from the slightest sound, and mister, you won't be able to hold your head high when he's finished with you. If you manage to kill him, I'll turn bounty hunter and hunt you down, just because I don't like you."

He closed the door behind him.

The men looked at one another and were slow to respond. In a short time, Lonergan crossed the floor and rushed outside, the former deputy was gone.

CHAPTER 22

Lonergan and Langford were standing in the middle on the main street of Lewisburg. They looked in every direction for a sign of Jones. None. Lonergan sighed, he alone knew the small man's abilities better than anyone, and the last thing he would have wanted, or even expected was looking down the barrel of his gun. Jones was a soft-spoken man, rarely did he speak out of turn, but he had laid his cards on the table. The former deputy had worked out what happened to Wilson. What else did he know? Fear consumed Lonergan as he ran to the Dusty Boot. Marlowe was standing behind the bar listening to a customer complaining about his lot in life. He welcomed the intrusion and moved from behind the bar to greet his friend. It was only when he was three feet away did he see the concern etched on his face.

The barkeep used his friend's first name. "What's wrong, Ed?"

Have you seen, Jones?"

"No, I haven't seen him since yesterday."

Lonergan withdrew his Peacemaker and climbed the stairs to his left. He knew Jones liked to spend his time with the whore, Rosa. He bounded the stairs quickly, while Marlowe watched on.

"Jones."

The first door on his left was locked so he put the heel of his boot to it just below the doorknob and it caved in instantly. A large woman and an equally large man looked up in fright.

"Jones."
He opened the door on his right and it was empty. The bed was unmade, and the room was a pigsty, but he crouched low and looked under the bed. Hearing footsteps he sprung to his feet and ran to the hall. Marlowe was standing at the top of the stairs. The whites of his eyes were large. Confusion swamped them and it took him longer than necessary to formulate the required words. "Jones is not here."
"Where's Rosa's room?"

He pointed, though his hand shook considerably. "Last door on the right."

Lonergan was quick to respond. He didn't knock or stop. Instead, Lonergan dropped his shoulder into the door and it collapsed under his weight and he fell to the floor. The Peacemaker fell from his grasp as he tried to protect himself, and it slid across the floor, hit the wall, and went off. A woman screamed. He scrambled to his feet and stooped to pick up his pistol. The embarrassment caused him to anger. "Where's that little runt, Jones?"

In a thick Spanish accent, she responded to the man's questions. "I haven't seen him since yesterday."

He holstered the gun and backhanded the whore across the face. "Where is he?"

Tears welled in her eyes. "Senor, I don't know where he is?"
"You liar." He holstered the gun and raised his hand and slapped the left side of her face with an open-handed slap. It would have made a grown man wince.

Rosa fell limp, though she was conscious. Her head was spinning, and tears rolled down her cheeks. It was a pitiful sight, but the rage of the sheriff could not be stemmed. "Tell me where he is, or so help me I'll."

"Ed. Let her go."

The man was in a rage and he turned to face the intruder.

Marlowe stared intensely. His friend's eyes were empty, yet afraid. He saw the anguish that tied him to his being. Who was he? The man he used to be was clinging to the last sinews of his moral self. His pupils were large and pleading. He needed help but would never ask for it. He was consumed with fear so profound and so longing that he threatened to yield to the passion that felt its way through his body and clung to every pore of his skin. The man had lost all sense of self and he was swimming in a sea of dread.

Marlowe stuttered. "Sh, sh, sh, she doesn't know, wh, wh, where he is."

Lonergan slapped her again and she stumbled backward, hit the end of the bed and fell to the floor where she cowered to protect herself from further assault. He reached out for the barkeep and grabbed him by the collar and jerked him forward at the same time he threw a straight right hand. The blow landed flush on Marlowe's nose. There was a sickening noise, like a whip cracking, and a god-awful scream. Blood flew in a wide arc as the gristle in the man's nose splintered and cracked under the force of the blow. Marlowe toppled backward and his head hit the floor hard and knocked him unconscious. Blood continued to spout like a geyser, painting the white walls red.

As Lonergan stepped around him Rosa, sensing the urgency of her benefactor's situation pulled a blanket off her bed. Evading the blood-red mist she managed to fold the material and place it over the man's face in a valiant attempt to stem the blood loss.

The lawman persisted in going through every room of the Dusty Boot in search of his prey. He pushed one man against the wall and threatened his life if he moved. He didn't move. In another room, he lifted the bed halfway off the ground with the couple still in it. He was a raging bull, and nothing would stop the rage besides time or a bullet. Making his way downstairs empty-handed, he went behind the bar and helped himself to a bottle and made his way to the mayor's private room. He drank greedily, kicked the door in, smashed the bottle on the bureau, and used the shards of the bottle to scar the furniture. He threw it against the mirror of the bureau when he finished, and it shattered. He returned to the barroom and the men scattered. They were unsure of what was wrong, but they didn't want to be in the way of the enraged lawman. He went behind the bar and grabbed another bottle of whiskey, pulled the cork out with his teeth, and spat it on the floor. He gulped greedily and burped. Wiping the back of his hand across his mouth, he called out again. "Jones."

Somewhere in the process of his rage, he had cut his left hand and it bled profusely. Blood ran onto his clothes and a dull red stain covered the left leg of his pants. By this time news of his antics had spread and the citizens of Lewisburg flocked to the Dusty Boot to see if the commotion was indeed caused by the man who had sworn to uphold the law. The citizens knew the man was unraveling. They could see it for the last twelve months. They had witnessed his demise. Since his brother died a few days ago he had turned to liquor to numb his pain. They were willing to forgive him for that if it didn't interfere with his job. Added to the confusion of the crowd was the news that the beloved Deputy Slick Jones had just been fired moments earlier.

Stepping through the batwings he was confronted with two dozen citizens who stood in the middle of the street. They were the law-abiding men and women of Lewisburg. They had no quarrels with the lawman, apart from questioning his character, and they watched him patiently as if demanding an explanation for his ruckus. The sheriff threw the bottle in the air and drew his Peacemaker and fired but the bottle fell hopelessly to the ground. The slug sailed over the heads of the onlookers and they ducked and ran for cover.

He looked straight across the street and saw the arrogant figure of Brett Langford. The man irked him. He had a way about him that Lonergan didn't like. It was time to teach the man a lesson. Half-way across the street, he saw movement out of his left eye. Turning he saw Ellery two hundred yards away. As much as he didn't like Langford, he hated Ellery even more. It was the way of people with money to expect the world to make way for them when they walked, to listen when they talked, despite how much nonsense they talked, and such men had a habit of such drivel. The most irksome trait of all was they, through polite convention and sweet hostility, expected others, those in need of their benefaction, to say "yes, sir' when they opened their check books.

Hearing the first gunshot, Ellery paused with his arms by his side. A statute of fear and adrenaline. He didn't mind gunplay when he was paying for it and wasn't around to witness it. He was the orchestrator of violence, but he rarely liked to know the details, preferring only to know that that job was complete. He took a few more steps and peered along the street and witnessed the crowd scatter. He was an exposed target and when Sheriff Lonergan stepped down off the steps of the Dusty Boot, he became frozen with fear. He didn't know what to think.

Lonergan squared up to Ellery and raised his Peacemaker, took a bead on the mayor right between the eyes, and fired. The distance was too great, and the slug whistled harmlessly short and fell to the ground. He smiled and continued to walk, albeit, somewhat staggeringly as the hangover from the night before accompanied by the healthy swigs of the whiskey were beginning to take their toll.

The mayor was rooted to the spot as Lonergan approached. The latter was unafraid, after all, he was the one with the gun. Fear can overcome a man until he realizes that the only thing, he has to lose is his life. That was the man's thinking as he raised his Peacemaker and fired. Once again, the slug fell short and kicked up a puff of dust. Still, he walked, and Ellery didn't move. Some of the onlookers believed the man was showing a pluck that most men didn't have, but he was just too scared to move. With every step, the lawman was getting closer to his target.

He was a hundred yards away.

Lonergan wouldn't waste another slug. The next time he pulled the trigger it would be a kill shot. The lives of both men had come down to this moment. From childhood to now. The journey of life through the highways and byways of lost opportunities and times forgotten. Of dreams unfulfilled, hope denied, and faith discarded. Where the memories of times past plagued them both and regret felt heavy in their hearts.

For Ellery, it was a story of deceit. His life was a lie. His name, his past, his wife, and his self-perceived importance was a misconstrued fantasy. He had it all yet was filled with discontent. Some men wanted to chase the sun, only as expected to always fall short of what they thought life owed them. They are replaceable, but they don't realize it until it's too late. They are no more than flesh and blood. Their importance is inflated and his view of himself is not how others see him. He strives for eternity in life, though never pausing to understand there is no such thing.

For the lawman, the time had come to pass. He had his opportunities to make something of his life. Indeed, he was once a man he was proud of. But pride is fleeting and its absence in a man is costly. It damages his soul. He questions his sense of self and he loses the meaning of, and connection to the world in which he lives. A weak man is a man without a tempered pride. He falls prey to the vagabonds that prey upon such men. He displays the character and vice of weak men. He drinks to excess. He abuses the weak in turn because he has been abused. He seeks power through exploiting others. He wanders the earth aimlessly and blames others for his failings. Such a man was Lonergan.

The crowd watched, much like they did days before when Thorn Hannon killed Will Lonergan in the exact spot where Ellery stood. If one was of a mind to look closely, they could still see the dried blood on the dust beneath the mayor's boots. Men and women craned their necks and shuffled along the boardwalk to watch the scene unfold. Regardless of their feelings for both men, they all agreed that watching a man shot down in cold blood was the most frightening thing they would ever witness. But it wasn't to be.

A tall man, with a rifle in his hands, stepped into the fray. He stepped soundly, but Ellery and Lonergan didn't hear or see him. As Lonergan stopped he began raising the Peacemaker and it fell from his grasp when the tall man brought the hilt of his Winchester down on the man's head. Lonergan fell to the ground in a crumpled heap. The men who considered Ellery courageous soon changed their tune when their gaze shifted due to the eyesight of old Peaty, the town drunk.

The man pointed and laughed, "Ellery done gone and wet himself."

The tension was broken, and the folks laughed.

CHAPTER 23

Thorn Hannon stood over the unconscious body of Sheriff Lonergan. He turned hastily and barked orders. "You and you, get over here and drag Lonergan to the jail. They responded, and as they grabbed him under the arms, Hannon reached down with his left hand and unpinned the badge, weighed it in his hand and put it in his pocket. Next, he picked up the Peacemaker and wedged it in his pants behind his belt.

The crowd was dispersing slowly and most of them went to the Dusty Boot to revel in the tales of what had happened.

Hannon followed the men as they dragged Lonergan to the jail where they tossed him in the cell. They were in a hurry to join the other men. He looked them up and down and pointed to the older man, "you stay." The other man exited the law office without another word.

The man who stayed was in his sixties and stooped slightly, but he was barrel-chested and strong. "Get the doctor, and then you can join your friends."
He was slightly confused. "Which doctor?"

"The closest one."

He nodded, 'Yes, sir."

Hannon found the keys to the cells after rummaging around for some time and clipped them to his belt. It wasn't the first time Thorn Hannon had to step up and take control of a situation. His experience as a Deputy in Drywater, a rough and tumble cattle town, had set him in good stead. It was a position he enjoyed and found it more to his liking than ranching. He figured his temperament suited such a field of employ, though he only ever talked about it with his fiancé. Deep down he harboured an urge to return to law enforcement.

A man in a fancy suit entered with a small leather bag in his right hand. He looked anxious. His face was long and somewhat worn. Hannon figured that it didn't matter what a person did for a living, all you had to do was look into their face. The difference between those that worked hard and those that didn't was plain to see. "Dubois, he's in the cell."

He nodded and tended to the patient, despite his misgivings about doing so.

Hannon woke early and planned to ride into town and have a word with Langford. He planned to find him and have a word with him about his ranch house burning down and the abuse of his fiancé. He hadn't expected to ride into the mess that the sheriff created. He didn't know what led up to the attempted shooting of the mayor, though he wanted to find out. All he knew, from murmurings, is that Lonergan fired Slick Jones moments before his rampage.

Rosa ran through the doors in a rush and both men turned. "Where's the doctor?"
Dubois stood and moved towards her. "What is it?"

"Marlowe has been hurt badly. He is upstairs at the saloon."

Dubois looked at Hannon and chucked a thumb over his shoulder. "He'll come around soon enough."

He followed Rosa out the door. Hannon watched them walk across the road and up the stairs and enter the saloon. To the left, he saw McGee and Thompson make their way across the street and pause. To their right, they waited for the banker Dobbins to reach them and the trio made their way to the jail.

The cell door slammed closed. He turned the key in the lock as Dobbins, McGee, and Thompson entered. It was McGee who took the floor and waited for Hannon to take a seat behind the desk. "Thorn. I sure am glad you showed up when you did."
He nodded. "Where's Slick?"
"Well, we don't rightly know. Elsa, Thompson's daughter, said she saw him riding out towards Lawnton."

It was then Dobbins took a step forward and stooped to pick up the Deputy's badge which was partly obscured under the desk and set it on the table.

It was the barber who spoke after he looked from his colleagues to Hannon and back again. "It appears as if Lewisburg is without a lawman."

McGee started to speak. "Thorn."

He stood, "no McGee."

His voice was pleading. "I know you were the Deputy of Drywater, until about a year ago."

"No."

"The town needs law and order Thorn and I'm going to come right out and say it. You're the best man for the job."

Thorn began to feel himself weaken. He wasn't a rancher. He was all lawman. He thought of Sarah and their future together. In their discussions about what it looked like, not once was it mentioned that he was a lawman again. "You just can't make me Sheriff. There are rules about such things."

Since the incident involving Lonergan and the mayor, Dobbins had been thinking of a way to distance himself from the latter. "Why not? There are three of the four members of the town council in this room. If all three of us decide it's appropriate to install you as Sheriff, until one is duly elected, then I'm sure the citizens of Lewisburg will find it reasonable."

McGee and Thompson nodded. A smattering of small talk ensued, and Hannon had to raise his voice to get them to pay attention.

"Gentlemen. Gentlemen. I came into town to confront a man who tried to have his way with Sarah. Slick Jones and Sarah are witnesses to the assault. Slick locked him up, but he is not here. I aim to see him punished."

McGee scratched his head and mused for a while, but Dobbins was quick-witted and responded sharply. "If Sarah says it happened then that's good enough for me. She has been a fine upstanding citizen her whole life. At least this way you'll be able to arrest him legally and let the courts work in your favor."

"What will people say?" McGee finished his musings. "The Hannon name is square in these parts. Your parents were well-liked and respected. Wade," he paused for effect, "God rest his soul, was a good man. There is not an honest man or woman in town that didn't hold him in high regard. The townsfolk will listen, Thorn and after what they witnessed today there can be no arguing that you're the best man for the job."

"If I accept, and I ain't saying I am, I want you to know that I will not use my position to settle a feud. This man has broken the law and I will bring him to justice. He will be treated like any other prisoner."

They nodded in agreement, but it was Dobbins who spoke. "You have the backing and the surety of the town council."

Thorn Hannon left home because he wanted to see the world, but at the heart of the decision was the realization that the ranching life wasn't for him. When he returned, he planned to settle a score, sell up and ride on, but he didn't count on the girl he knew as little Sarah being all grown up and unmarried.

"All right. I'll accept the position on one condition."
"What will it be, Thorn?"

"Sarah's home alone. I want you to organize some men to protect her while I chase this Langford character down. I have reason to believe he burned my ranch down. He took the note out of his pocket and handed it to Dobbins who read it and passed it to his companions.

"I found this note stuck to the barn door. The house Ma and Pa built was burned to the ground."
McGee whistled softly. "Bertie," his son "and Sarah went to school together. He has been hankering to get away from the store for a while. Are you happy with that decision, Thorn?"

"McGee, Bertie is a good man. Sarah will enjoy his company."

"Is that a yes?"

Hannon nodded. "It's a yes."

Thorn removed the badge from his pocket and pined it to his shirt. "Isn't there an oath or something?"
McGee looked to Thompson and back to Dobbins. "Do you want to be Sheriff or not?"

"Yeah, I reckon I do."

"Then Sheriff Hannon, I'll be seeing you."

McGee turned and headed towards the door but stopped when Ellery walked into the room. The mayor of Lewisburg tried to walk with a firm step, but he failed.

When he spoke he tried to with bravado but failed. His voice was weak and high pitched. "What's going on here?"

McGee couldn't hide his disgust. Even though Ellery had come close to being shot down in cold blood, he reasoned that two men knew exactly why that was and that was Lonergan and Ellery. "Hannon has been sworn in as Sheriff until a suitable replacement can be found."

Ellery looked aghast. "That can't be. It's against the charter of the council."

Dobbins laughed. He knew the law better than anyone. His tone was condescending, "Chapter seven, Article six states that in an emergency, such as the death of a Sheriff or Deputy, the town council, buy a majority decision has the power to elect a lawman to act as an interim officer of the peace until such times as the situation can be remedied."

"But."
Thompson stepped forward. "It seems to me you have an unnecessary grievance with Mr. Hannon. I find that strange Lloyd, considering he just saved your life."

He tried to find the words, but they weren't forthcoming. He stuttered and blubbered but nothing resembling any sense emanated from his dry lips.

Dobbins persisted. "I request an urgent town council meeting for tonight. There are matters to discuss."

"Agreed," said Thompson. McGee just nodded his acceptance.

It was Dobbins again. "seven o'clock at the bank. Sheriff, you are entitled to be there, and I expect you will not let us down."

McGee excused himself. "Pardon me gentlemen, Lloyd. Thorn, I mean Sheriff, Bertie will leave directly."

The three notable men of Lewisburg filed out after one another and Ellery was left standing by the door. He looked over his shoulder to make sure no one was watching and then approached the newly crowned Sheriff. He had been humiliated by Lonergan and the other members of the town council went behind his back and now they were moving to oust him as mayor. That's why the meeting was being held. He knew that much, but he wouldn't give up without a fight. He found some courage and his back straightened.

"I don't like you, Hannon."

"It'll be Sheriff Hannon to you."

He smirked. "I always get my way."

"Is that so?"

"That's right Mr. Lawman and I'll tell you exactly what I want?"

"What's that?"

"I will own your ranch and then I will own the McKinnon spread. I don't care what I have to do to get it?"

Thorn stepped into the man and Ellery had to take a step back to stare up at him. He smiled and laughed.

"What's so damn funny, Hannon?"

"Wait till Lonergan comes around. Don't forget he tried to kill you, so I figure he won't be too reluctant to talk."

The look on the mayor's face was priceless. The newly crowned Sheriff picked him up by the shirt collar and carried him to the door where he laid a book into the man's backside and sent him careening into the street where he fell into the dust.

The mayor of Lewisburg stood and tried to brush himself off before making haste.

Hannon stepped into the late morning and headed for the Dusty Boot. Though the day was young the place was full. He stepped through the crowd and forced his way to the bar. Rosa was walking back and forth taking orders as best she could.

"How's Marlowe?"

The look of concern on her face was real. "The doctor said he'll be sore for a while, but that he needs rest."

"Tell Marlowe, I'll be by to check on him later on."

He turned to face the patrons and one man, then the next saw the star on his chest and a general silence, after a few mutterings and muffled whispers, descended on the room. He found the barrel-chested man he was looking for and signaled for him to go outside. The man in question downed his drink and moved through the crowd towards the exit. He figured it was the right time to tell them exactly what he thought.

"My name's Thorn Hannon and I'm the new Sheriff. I'm a reasonable man. Abide by the law and we'll get along just fine."
He made it halfway to the door before the crowd erupted in a cheer.

He met the older man on the front step. "What's your name stranger?"

His voice was gravelly. "Tucker Johns, but most folks just call me Tuck."

"Well, Tuck. I'm a reasonable judge of character and I'd like to offer you a job."

He was interested, "What would I have to do?"

"Sit at the jailhouse and if anyone comes in acting foolish and trying to free or harm the prisoner, shoot them."

"Just like that."

"That's right."

The man considered it an honor, "I'm your man."

"Excellent. Do you own a gun, or do I have to find one for you?"

"I'm sorted."

"Good meet me at the jail as soon as you can."

CHAPTER 24

Mrs. Ellery was a woman on a mission. She sat at her desk and wrote feverishly. Her mind was made up. She was returning to Boston, and she was taking Maude with her. Her husband could die for all she was concerned about. She had long forgotten what it was like to love a man so shallow and weak. Was it ever love? No. It wasn't. She thought that perhaps in time she would come to care about her husband, as a wife must, but she had tried and when she knew she never could, she turned to drink to numb the pain. Oh, how she despised him. There was no shred of masculinity in him. She had never felt so much distaste for the man that shared her bed. The dislike had been evident for many years, it's just that he didn't read the signals. She either refused to acknowledge them or was trying to fool herself, that in the end, it would be all okay. But '*the end*,' was some time away and she wasn't waiting anymore. He was clueless of her true intentions and she had been afraid to act on them. She did not know why she suddenly felt this way, only that she did. She had wasted her youth away and though she was past her prime she planned to make the most of the time she had left, while her looks and form held. When she finished writing the letter, she folded it and stuck it in an envelope and held it out for the girl.

"Do you know the banker?"
"Yes ma'am, his name is Dobbins."

"Excellent. Take this note to the bank and give it directly to him. Don't give it to anyone else."

"Yes, Mrs. Ellery."

She shivered at the name, but there was nothing she could do about that, yet. She opened the drawer of her desk and rummaged around and came out with a key. She held it out for the girl who reached for it warily. "Lock the back door on your way out and lock it when you return. Hand Dobbins the note and come straight back." Maude nodded eagerly and left the room.

The woman took a deep breath and penned another letter. This one was more meaningful and longer. The words were filled with spite and anger. The thoughts and feelings she had kept bottled up for years came gushing out. The more she wrote the angrier the letter became. She stopped writing and moved across to the bureau and filled a glass full of gin. She gulped the liquor and the bitter taste caused her to wince with her mouth open. The look on her face was one of frustrated determination. Leaving her husband was an easy decision, but sometimes decisions can be difficult to enact upon. Even to her detriment, she had stayed in a loveless marriage. She had soured and had given up on life too soon. Finishing the drink, she poured another and moved back to the desk and continued her letter.

Writing feverishly, she paused every so often to contemplate the right words. She wished her husband would die and cursed him for the life he had carved out for her. What man would drag his wife across the country in a vain pursuit of fame and fortune? She was compliant and played her part well, but she was unwilling to abide by the tenets of her wifely duties any longer.

She folded the letter neatly and put it in an envelope on which she simply wrote, Lloyd. Grabbing it in her hand she moved swiftly across the room and down the stairs. Opening the door, she wedged the end of the envelope under the mat. Closing the door, she locked it and returned to the upstairs room.

It the silence that followed she contemplated the difficulties of traversing the rugged landscape back to Boston. She reversed the trip that initially brought them to Lewisburg. It was three days' travel on the train and two by stage. Allowing time for minor delays, she and Maude, for which she had a quiet affection, would be in Boston a week from now. The thought pleased her. If her message to Dobbins fared well, she would return a wealthy woman.

On her return to the city, she would re-establish herself and Maude at her father's residence. He would accept her. He would make a scene, but he would welcome her into his life again.

The back door opened and closed, and she could hear the key in the lock. The short yet steady trop of the girl could be heard.

"Maude."

The girl entered the room. "Yes ma'am."

Margaret Ellery moved across to the edge of the bed and sat. She tapped the mattress next to her and Maude sat, reservedly. "Maude, we will be leaving for Boston as soon as I make the arrangements. I won't be coming back to Lewisburg. I would like you to come with me. If you wish to return, I will pay your fare. I know you have family here and moving so far away is a big decision, but it is one you have to make. I need to know."

The girl started the cry. Tears fell down her face, but she refused to wipe them away. "My mama doesn't care about me, Mrs. Ellery."

"Now, now, I'm sure that's not true."
"Is too. Every time I go home, she holds out her hand and says "where is it? When I give her the money, she treats me as if I'm not there."

"What about your brothers and sisters?"

She ignored the question. Maude had promised herself that she would do whatever had to be done to live a poverty-free existence. She felt no loyalty to her family. She had a dream on more than one occasion. It was her future. Life in Lewisburg wasn't to be in it, neither was her family. "Mrs. Ellery, I would like to go to Boston with you. I've heard it's such a nice place."

She kissed the girl on the top of the head. "Well, we better start packing. We will be traveling light. That means one case, so we better make it a big one."

Maude laughed. She was docile, but a dreamer. The world was a big place and she wanted to experience her share of it.

CHAPTER 25

Ellery knew the town council meeting to be held that night was to remove him from his position. He wasn't going to go and plead his case to men who had already made their mind up. It was a waste of everyone's time. He was to go home and seek comfort and advice from his wife. His stride was long and in a short time, he managed to cover quite some distance. He did not look up once, but he could hear the laughter and the murmuring as he walked. He could not bear to look anyone in the eye. As he walked, he cussed. He cussed Lonergan for all he was and all he was ever going to be. The man may hang, at the very least he will be sent to jail. The thought wasn't as comforting as he hoped.

All that he had worked hard for was on the brink of collapse and it was all his fault. It was because he didn't know people as well as he thought he did. Ellery knew how to handle money. He had a keen business mind and used this to his advantage by exploiting anyone he could to meet the desired outcome. Profit equaled purpose. But his failure was people. Sure, he could trade on other people's motivations and buy them if need be, but he assumed that at the heart of all men and women was a desire for wealth and economic growth. But people are not markets, and they respond to the peaks and troughs of their life with emotions. In turn, these influenced their relations with others. If he had taken time to learn anything from his father-in-law, before he embezzled a large sum of money, it was that you needed to build relations. It does not matter if they are real or not. In many cases, it is a lie, but people must believe that they matter. If he had paid Lonergan the money he owed him and grieved a little with him when his brother was killed, then he wouldn't be in this situation. Ellery didn't see it like that of course. He was looking too far into the future. It was the same as constructing a building without adequate foundations. The building will fall.

He cussed Peaty, the town drunk, for pointing out his accident. He had never been so scared and if Thorn Hannon didn't have the courage, to handle Lonergan the way he did, he would be dead. The moment in which he felt obliged to the new sheriff had passed. He held nothing for contempt for him. In a short time, he had fallen a long way. He was bound to be replaced as mayor. He would never recover from his disgrace. It was in his best interest to leave Lewisburg, change his name again, and start over. There was to be no other course of action.

He stopped walking and considered Lonergan. What if he was talking? What if he was at that moment telling Hannon everything he knew. Dread grasped hold of him, and he quickened his stride. He opened the gate of his home and as soon as he stepped into the yard, he felt safer. Climbing the stairs, he went to open the door but found it locked. He tried again. There must be some mistake. He called out "Maude."

There was no response and hanging his head in anger, he wiped his feet on the mat when he saw the envelope. He picked it up and removed the letter. It was long so he sat on the top step to read it.

Lloyd

What I write I do so with a clear mind and a conviction, with which I have rarely displayed throughout our marriage. I despise you. I have for many years now. I can't recall exactly when or why I started harboring these feelings, but they are real. You are weak-willed and fragile. In your infinite wisdom, you brought me to the end of the earth, to this god-awful place to make your fortune, but you will fail. It is in your nature to do so. I am leaving and returning home. Father is expecting me. I have been in correspondence with him, for well over a year now.

You will never see me again, as I have no desire to be in your presence. You sicken me. I have played the role expected of me all these years, but my loyalty has not been repaid in kind. I will never forgive you for your infidelity, nor will I stand by and let you bring me down. You are not man enough to tame my passions. Your touch disgusts me. You have brought enough shame on my name and I will not tolerate this abuse any longer. I am taking what is left of my father's money and what few possessions I have acquired throughout our union. Everything you have bought me will be left behind. I have no desire to remember you. Maude will be my traveling companion and I look forward to removing her from this wretched place.

I would say goodbye, but that would imply some affection for you, of which I have none. Instead, I will leave our parting with a question and I care not about your response, but you should.

Do you need an excuse to be a man?

Margaret

He stared with disbelief and stood hastily and started banging on the door.

"Maude, open the door."

Mrs. Ellery stood with her arm around Maude behind the curtain of the upstairs window. The young girl was scared, but she took comfort in the women's resolve. They listened for five minutes as Ellery yelled out and banged on the door. The passers-by, aware of what had happened moments earlier, were quick to lend an ear to the profanities that the mayor was yelling out.

Dwayne Foreman, a genial man with a sound disposition, was riding past when he heard the commotion. He felt obligated to remind the mayor of his responsibilities as a husband. "Excuse me, sir."

Ellery turned in a huff. "What do you want?"

Foreman was quick to respond. "A husband doesn't speak to his wife in that manner."

The mayor turned and spat the words out in anger. "This has nothing to do with you, Foreman." The man dismounted and opened the gate. "The whole street can hear your profanities and as I said, a man doesn't speak to a woman in that manner, especially his wife."

The smaller man walked down the stairs and stared up at the window where he knew his wife would be watching him. He looked Foreman up and down as he walked past. Without saying another word, he turned and ran down the street. He needed to see Dobbins.

Foreman looked up at the window and the curtain parted. Mrs. Ellery smiled and waved in appreciation.

He closed the gate and nodded. Mounting, he continued his journey, though he added a destination because he felt that the new Sheriff needed to know exactly what had happened.

CHAPTER 26

The mayor sat at the kitchen table across from Bernice Lonergan. He had just finished telling her what had happened, though an acquaintance of hers had visited earlier to inform her about her father. She was devastated by the news, though not surprised. She was concerned about her father, but not enough to visit him, after all, he had tried to kill the love of her life and she hated him for that. She looked at Ellery with blind devotion and hung on every word he said. She believed him of course, after all, they were in love and he would not lie to her.

The man was distraught. It was a day to forget, but one that would never be forgotten. Not only had he been humiliated by the former Sheriff and Peaty the town drunk, but his wife had also deserted him when he needed her most. He knew the importance of the woman in his life and he just assumed that she would be willing to spend her life in his shadow as he bumbled from one town and deal to another in search of what he needed most, respect. The man craved it, but instead of working for it, he tried to buy it. It never works. Men like him who had tried the same thing since time immemorial had been ignorant in the same regard. There is nothing more wholesome and purer than that which is earned. He did not understand the importance of such things and through ignorance had based his life on assumptions. As a result, he had always avoided taking responsibility. He ended up creating a weak version of himself, founded on mistruths and false expectations of others. He had become lazy and inconsiderate. This led to the development of bad habits. It was a downward spiral and he deserved everything he got.

Bernice felt hopeless. She reached across the table to grab his hands, but he rejected her touch. Damn her father to hell for what he had done. To hell with Peaty who had spent his life searching for answers in a bottle, only to humiliate the man she loved. The only person she wasn't angry at was Mrs. Ellery. She was grateful. Now they could be together.

Ellery's meeting with Dobbins didn't go as planned. His wife had withdrawn all the money that was owed her from their joint account, opened one in her name, and deposited it forthwith. Dobbins followed all the instructions in the note. She withdrew not one cent more than was taken from her father. That she still left him with a sizable sum and the deeds to land he acquired after he arrived in town, was a testament to her virtue, but he didn't consider it that way. The transaction was conducted, honorably as far as Dobbins was concerned. Though to the inquisitive, his desire to see the end of Ellery was behind every move he made. It was how certain men responded when one of their kind had been caught out doing something wrong. It was about rescuing one's reputation and distancing oneself from the wrongdoer. Dobbins was acting as expected. Ellery would have done the same thing if the situation were reversed.

Ellery considered making a grandiose display of honor but knew such a stand could prove more fatal than helpful, as his wife may be willing to use certain information against him. In his anger, he imagined killing her but knew he didn't have the stomach for it. But, when Rick Cleaver appeared, things would change. Yes, Cleaver was the answer to his problems. The gunman would take care of Hannon and Lonergan. When the smoke settled on that score, he would consider keeping the man around. Considering this, he smiled, and his mood lightened. His mind worked overtime, and he began formulating a plan to restore his credibility. He was honor-bound to do so. His initial response involved disappearing in the middle of the night, and soon. On reflection, this would prove his guilt. Gossip and innuendo would follow him wherever he went. It was best to stay and weather the storm. With Rick Cleaver in his corner, revenge would be assured.

He, in turn, reached across the table and stared into the lovesick eyes of Bernice Lonergan. "Do you have a pencil and paper?"
Without a word, she rummaged through the drawers until she found the requested items. "Here you go."

"Thanks, Bernie." It was his name for her, and she liked it.

"What are you doing?"

"I'm resigning as Mayor,"
She was shocked, "but."

He put the forefinger of his right hand to his lips to silence her. "If we are going to be together then you must learn that if I need advice, I will ask you for it. Until then, I'd appreciate it if you let me take care of business."

She was not offended. Instead, she just smiled and said, "of course, I'll make you a cup of tea."

The man had learned nothing. He would hang onto Bernice. She was attractive enough; besides she would do until he managed to find someone else. He penned his resignation in silence and drank from the teacup when pausing to consider how to proceed. When the letter was finished he folded it and thought about placing it in the pocket of his shirt, but it was only then that he realized that he was still in the same clothes in which he had an accident.

"Bernie."
She flitted in from the other room, eager to be of assistance. "Yes."

"I don't seem to have any clothes. Would you be a darling and go to Mrs. Brady and pick up three shirts, pants, undergarments, and socks? She knows my size. After all, I can't possibly go out looking like this."

"Most certainly."

"Tell her to put it on my tab."

She moved swiftly and responded in the affirmative before waving goodbye and exiting promptly.

He took another sip of tea. It was divine.

CHAPTER 27

Langford watched the events unfold before his very eyes. The antics of the former sheriff amused him. The day he met him; he could tell the man was heading for a fall from grace. He had seen it too many times, for the signs not to be obvious. His father had displayed many of the signs before he was mutilated in a hail of lead. It was a combination of the drunkenness, offset by a tragedy of some sort, and other multiplying factors. He found it amusing. As far as he was concerned, Lonergan was a fool and deserved to hang. It was left up to Slick Jones to make Lonergan accountable and he did, to some extent. But it was obvious the former Deputy was onto something and that was why he was fired. He wasn't that unhappy that Slick Jones had, by all accounts, skipped town. He didn't like him and if their paths crossed again then one of them would die. He was sure of that.

During the former Sheriff's rampage, Langford watched. At first from across the street and then as a patron of the Dusty Boot and lastly as he lost himself in the crowd, watching from a distance. He had his back to Hannon when he walked past and stepped onto the porch. He pushed his way through the onlookers and only became aware of the man's identity when he clubbed Lonergan. He was spoken of admirably and with a mark of respect. Such talk displeased him unless it was about him, then he was all for it.

The mayor wetting himself was the funniest thing he had seen in a while. He had seen it many times before. Men get consumed with fear and something happens to them and they lose all control. He didn't know exactly, but every time it happened it brought laughter and derision from the onlookers. In retrospect, it wasn't always fair to judge a man on how he must confront such a challenge. In his experience, often men were brave enough, just a mite foolish and it was this foolishness that brought them undone. A man can learn to confront fear, indeed embrace it, but for most men, it isn't natural and the man that controls his response is usually the one who comes out the victor.

He watched the way Hannon moved and he was impressed. He had learned to respect his adversaries. It was the first lesson his father taught him. A man must always be wary of every person that crosses his path. People were unpredictable and gave the impression that they were incompetent, but even such men have a way of surprising you. The buffoons, the lazy, and the frightened have a threshold to which they will be willing to be pushed before they stand their ground. Hannon was none of these types of men. He was a cut above. He listened to the saloon talk by saloon men, they were his breed. They spoke of Hannon admirably. Some were surprised by the man's conversion to lawman but those that claimed to know him best felt he was the perfect man for the job. Langford had heard stories in Drywater about the Deputy of that very city. Not long after his brother, Charlie was killed he skipped town. No-one knew for sure where. But he chased down every lead until eventually, he heard the name Hannon spoken of in a saloon in Wheeling, West Virginia. The man spoke of Wade Hannon. The storyteller, after a round or two was shared, was content to tell the story of the man's murder. It seems he was passing through Lewisburg when the murder occurred. He had no idea who the man was talking to and the man in question knew little, other than the story he told. He had chased leads down before, and they had led to nothing, but he knew his luck would hold eventually.

He listened, he watched, and he waited, but the time was near, oh so near when Langford would confront the newly crowned Sheriff of Lewisburg. It was hard to explain the difficulties of sitting in the back corner of the saloon keeping out of mischief. He was able to when he put his mind to it. It was hard though, as a drunk fell over and bumped the table, which spilled his drink. Normally, such an incident would have resulted in the man copping a beating, and deservedly so. Langford bit his tongue and accepted the man's apology.

Time passed slowly. Langford waited patiently. It was almost time. He could taste it. He was almost salivating. He was ready.

Hannon pushed through the batwings and the men fell silent. He walked straight up the stairs and once out of sight the men regained their composure. Langford waited. The moment had arrived. He would kill the man who murdered his brother and keep his promise to his dying mother. He couldn't help but smirk at the thought of the confrontation. He discarded his brother, but an image of his mother came to him. It was the moment before her death. He recalled her dying words, "promise me, son."

He felt a sense of pride overwhelm him as he recalled his response, "I will, Mama."

Two minutes later Hannon walked down the stairs. The Sheriff's badge stood out in the dim room. Men made way for him. They offered courtesies just to engage the man in conversation.

Langford stood and rolled his shoulders and stepped forward.

The lawman left the saloon, Langford was not far behind him.

Hannon was half-way across the street when he heard the challenge.

"Thorn Hannon."

The new Sheriff turned. It was the man he was after. As soon as he saw the stranger, he knew he was in a tussle. Everything about him smelled tough. His stance. His long face. Weathered skin and that look of death in his eyes. "You'd be, Brett Langford?"
"That's right. I have got a score to settle with you. Then again, I figure you already know that."

Standing before him was the man who abused his fiancé and burned down his family home. He felt an instant rage but knew acting on it would prove foolish. The man standing before him was no choirboy. His eyes rested on the sidearm on the man's hip. "I ain't carrying."
The onlookers had gathered like ants to honey.

"For what I'm planning I don't need a gun."

"Is that so?"
"That's right, Hannon. Give the word and I'll disarm right now."

Hannon wasn't going to let him leave. He didn't want to be let go. He was staying. He unpinned the badge and put it in his pocket. His words were enough to quell the muffling of the men and women who watched on earnestly. "This is personal, and I won't hide behind the badge to settle the score. If I fall, the man is free to go." Langford smiled. It was thin and telling. The man himself had been waiting for this moment for a long time. He had dreamed about it. Envisioned it. He undid the holster and hung it over the post at the end of the steps. "You murdered my brother."

Hannon squared up to the man who approached and stopped five feet away. "Your brother was no good. There's nothing lower than a man that lays his hands on a woman. You're low Langford. The worst kind of man."

"I know who and what I am, Sheriff. I sleep at night."

"I'm sure you do."

Both men eyed one another coldly. They sought their revenge against the actions of the other. Rightly or wrongly both men were honor-bound to act. The challenger was loyal and courageous. He was rugged and determined. His oath to a dying mother never far from his thoughts. He had carried the burden for the last year and now, in Lewisburg Pennsylvania, he was getting his chance to remedy the injustice done to the Langford name. The newly crowned lawman sought redemption. He and his fiancé had been wronged. He would not rest until the abuser was held to account. The man had occupied his thoughts, day, and night. It had only been a few days but felt much longer. It gave him an insight into how desperate Langford was. He hoped this desperation caused the man to act rashly. But he could tell that the critter standing across from him was not the type.

"I could have shot you a dozen times and left town without anyone knowing it was me."
"Then why didn't you?"

"I want to watch the life drain from your eyes when I deliver the killing blow."

"There's nothing left to be said."

Both men circled to their left and back to the right looking for an opening.

The challenger moved forwards and jabbed twice and threw a straight right which broke through Hannon's defenses and caught him just above his left eye. The blow stung but he was sick of backpedalling and evaded the man's next blow, stepped to his left, and moved forward with a flurry of his own. Both men repositioned themselves and advanced and backpedalled, throwing punches, and searching for an opening. The defenses were solid. Their footing was sound, and it would take a mighty blow to dislodge them. They searched for a weakness in one another. The dust kicked up about their feet as they shuffled across the earth. The fighting circle moved in and out with the action.

Hannon connected with a solid combination and Langford could taste blood in his mouth. Despite the punches, Langford countered quickly when Hannon dropped his arms and a straight right-hand connected flush. They continued to watch one another as they both spat blood into the street. Hannon jabbed with his left and tried an uppercut, but he missed the man's chin by the width of a piece of paper. The effort he threw into the punch caused him to lose balance and Langford pounced. He threw an overhand right that sounded like two bulls butting heads and Hannon felt every ounce of pressure in the blow and fell to one knee. The crowd jeered. Their champion had suffered a mighty blow.

He stood straight up but Langford sensing his opportunity advanced quickly. As he stood, he staggered backward and lost his balance. Another flurry of blows, though not one of them connected flush, caused Hannon to fall again. The crowd was not happy. They feared for the worst and rightly so. The lawman's adversary was unrelenting.

He rolled quickly to his left to evade the man's assault. It was a smart move, as a boot came crashing down right where his face was a split second ago.

Langford laughed, sneered, and advanced. He backed the lawman up ten yards, twenty yards. The blows were quick, but his defense was solid. Hannon backed away until his retreat was stopped by a wagon. He was cornered and fought like his life depended on it because it did. He charged his attacker and caught him in an awkward embrace, and they landed hard in the dirt. They rolled around grappling for an advantage, both men knew that each had their strong points. Hannon had no chance against the man on his feet. But as they wrestled, he could tell that his strength was superior, and it allowed him to gain the edge he needed. Hannon straddled his foe and pinned his right arm to the ground with his left knee and unleashed a sickening blow if it would have connected. At best it was a glancing blow, as he moved his head to avoid the onslaught. Langford raised his hips off the ground and twisted to his right and cast his attacker off him. Both men rushed back to their feet but paused a moment to catch their breath.

Hannon lunged again but Langford was prepared and stepped aside. The latter advanced swinging hefty blows, however, they were erratic attempts and the lawman managed to land a straight right that caught the attacker on the point of the chin, and he buckled slightly at the knees. Hannon felt the man give way underneath the force of the blow. It was Langford's turn to backpedal, but his defense was strong. Except for a blow that skimmed off the top of his head, he had managed to withstand the barrage. The men were tired as they left nothing to chance. Their hands were low, and Langford jabbed twice and connected flush with the right. A left hook snapped his head back the other way, but Hannon's chin and stance were strong. A right hook was easily evaded by the Sheriff and as he ducked, he lunged. His right shoulder catching Langford underneath the arm. He lifted as he continued his surge forward and drove the man into the ground. A rush of wind and a loud noise emanated from Langford as his back was driven into the hard ground. Hannon straddled him again and unleashed with a right and then left.

The crowd rose with their champion but soon died when the prone man reached out his hand and poked Hannon in the eyes. His eyes watered immediately, and Langford scrambled to safety. He stood and kicked Hannon in the ribs. The latter went with the impact and rolled over onto his back. Langford stepped closer to drive the heel of his boot down on his opponent's face. Once again, Hannon managed to avoid the attack, roll to his right and stand. He was met with a series of punches that snapped his head back. A left hook wobbled his knees and a right uppercut picked the man up and dropped him heavily in the dirt. He tried to rise but was kicked in the ribs again. He thought he heard something snap. Hannon was in trouble. He had never fought such a ferocious opponent. The man was relentless, a hard case with years of experience. He began to doubt himself. He told himself to stand, but it all seemed too hard. He struggled to breathe, and his lungs burned. His mouth was bleeding and his left eye was swollen. He had never been manhandled like this before. In all his years he had seen his adversaries off with little to no fuss, but the man called Langford was unlike anyone else he had ever confronted. He saw the man's face looking over him, he couldn't make out what was said as the man hurled insults at him. The crowd rose again. Their muffled chant getting louder and louder. Langford looked over his shoulder. He sensed dread. He needed to leave and quickly. Still, there was a matter of the promise he made. He must keep his word. As he stared at Hannon, he had a begrudging respect for him. He disliked him, but that had nothing to do with respect. The crowd moved closer and instead of going in for the kill he scurried twenty yards and removed his Colt from his tan holster. He waved it around and the men departed. They had a soft spot for Hannon, but they weren't willing to take a bullet for him.

Hannon rolled to his knees. He was breathing heavily. Langford walked slowly to the lawman and the indistinguishable sound of the hammer being pulled into position felt heavy on the air. Some men turned away, unable to watch what was about to happen, others leaned closer, not wanting to miss a moment of the cold-blooded execution.

The gunman stopped five feet short of the lawman. Just out of reach of any sudden lunge. He straightened his back and looked from left to right. He was tired and hurting, but he had triumphed. He always won. He spat when he spoke. "Any last words, lawman?" Hannon spat blood. "Go to hell, Langford."

He raised the Colt and smiled. Looking along with the site, he stared into the eyes of his brother's killer. Hannon looked up at his maker, prepared to stare death in the face. Langford's words were loud enough for all to hear. "Honor can bring a man peace, or it can destroy him. There's nothing in between." "Langford."

He whirled quickly, spotted his target, and raised the Colt. But that was as far as he got. Slick Jones pulled the trigger and lead whistled through the air and made a sickening thud, not once but twice. The shots were fired in such quick procession that the debate of how many bullets he fired raged well into the night. The first leaden intruder punctured hit him in the middle of the chest and the second came to rest an inch below the first. Langford fell awkwardly. His left leg tucked underneath his right when he fell. The Colt spilling from his grasp. He lolled his head to his left and stared into the face of Hannon and uttered his dying words before closing his eyes for the last time, "I'm sorry, Mama."

CHAPTER 28

The day after the violence a solemn mood settled over the citizens of Lewisburg. The day of violence, unlike any other, had come and gone. The reasons behind Lonergan's attempted murder of Ellery and Thorn Hannon's ascension to Sheriff were reasonable grounds for inquiry. Add to that, the man named Langford, who manhandled the lawman, was gunned down by the ex-lawman, Slick Jones. There were also rumors that Ellery had resigned as mayor. It was too much to understand. They needed clarification. They needed answers and they needed to know that the violence was going to end.

The previous evening was spent in quiet revelry. The violence weighed heavily on their minds. Some men discussed the turn of events in romantic terms. They relived the day repeatedly. They imagined themselves as the hero and the more they drank the more courageous they became. A few fights broke out at the Dusty Boot and the lawmen of Lewisburg were quick to respond. Slick Jones had been reinstated as Deputy by the remaining members of the town council and was accepted readily by a grateful Thorn Hannon.

Some men and women preferred to discuss such happenings with a sober mind. They sat around the fire or the kitchen table with their loved ones and discussed the events with an impartial mind. Talk fluctuated, but it was held in the comfort and warmth of a home designed to keep them safe from the troubles of the outside world. It was in such a place that inquisitive children asked their parents questions they had no answer for. It was at times a cruel world and the parents tried to allay the fears of the youth while seeking answers to their questions.

Not all citizens were occupied with the violence that fell upon the town. There were those like Margaret Ellery and Maude who abhorred it and found no comfort in its discussion. They spent the night packing and Maude listened to stories of life in Boston. The more she listened the more questions she asked. She was an inquisitive child, full of hopes and dreams. The smile in the girl's eyes made Mrs. Ellery feel alive. She felt young again. The persistence of youth matures with time, but it never truly disappears. We paint our picture and we alone determine its color. Some erase parts of it and then others add to its form and shape. In the end, we see the world not only through the eyes of the person who we have become but also in part, from the person we used to be.

The stage was due at any moment. They were the only passengers embarking from Lewisburg. Henry, the telegraph operator, was having a slow day and he tried his best to engage the women in conversation, but they were having no part of it. Once again, rumors persisted that Mrs. Ellery was leaving and had sworn never to return. The former mayor was not welcome. Besides, he had spent his time in isolation with Miss. Lonergan. It was a scandal of the highest order.

"Have you ever been on a train before, Maude?"

"No ma'am. I've never left Lewisburg."

"You poor child. I guess you do not know this because of your youth but staying in one place too long can kill the will to live. It numbs your sense of adventure. You learn to prefer comfort to travel and contentment to new experiences. The air you breathe becomes stale. You eat the same meals and have the same conversations with the same people. Life becomes mundane and routine. You fall into a rhythm with life and you tick out your time meandering from one expectation to another. Such a life is for those that are afraid to embrace the majesty and beauty of life. They know no better because they refuse to dream and even if they do, they do not know how to act upon them. Men and women, it does not matter which, live life to a preordained script. It is different for them all and even women have certain expectations foisted upon them. It depends on one's status. It is dependent on age and wealth. We are so cruel to one another, Maude, but we are so much harsher to ourselves. We deny ourselves the experiences that make us the people we truly can be. What is life but the application of ourselves to it?"

She loved how the woman talked, though she only ever understood some of what the woman said. "Yes, ma'am."

"Oh Maude, you are so innocent and sweet. Can you remember something for me please?"
"I will do my best, Mrs. Ellery."

She smiled sincerely. "Don't let life get in the way of yourself."
"I'm sorry ma'am. I don't rightly understand."

She put her arm around the girl's shoulder. "Forget about it, Maude. Perhaps when you are older, it will make more sense."
She was about to continue the conversation when the door of the waiting room opened, and Lloyd Ellery walked into the room.

She looked from the girl to the man she was leaving and said. "I would like you to call me Mrs. Tyler, after all, that is my maiden name."

Maude saw the man approach. "Do you want me to leave?"
He went to respond in the affirmative, but the woman cut him off. "Maude, please stay."

There was an awkward silence. The woman stared at her husband with a gaze that could melt ice. Maude looked to the floor. She was uncomfortable and felt out of place.

Ellery was struggling to come up with the right words. His voice was muffled and slightly incoherent. "Is there any chance you would consider staying?"

She was condescending. "No."

"But."

"There are to be no buts. I have no more time for you. Go back to that," she paused for effect and looked him up and down, "hussy. Get out of my sight."

"Margaret, I'm sorry."

She stood and advanced toward him and he cringed slightly. She stared into his eyes. He was lonely and afraid. He was empty and carrying the burden of sorrow deep within. She laughed, but it quickly turned to anger. "You're pathetic."
Ellery reached out for his wife, and she unleashed with a sickening slap on the man's left cheek. It brought tears to his eyes and they spilled over the edge.

The door opened and Henry stood there nervously. "The stage is coming."

Mrs. Tyler, as she now liked to be called, grabbed Maude by the hand, and left the room without a word.

The stage jutted to a halt. The smell of sweat and leather filled the air. An average looking man stepped down off the driver's box and opened the door. "Two ladies stepped into the day. They were young and relatively pretty. The driver was overly nice to them. Mrs. Tyler considered them whores and had no time for them. She waited patiently, as the driver was distracted by their ineptness.

In the time that the Ellery's had been in Williamstown they had been invited to many dinner parties and had lots of acquaintances, but no friends. The news that the lady was returning to Boston had spread far and wide, but no one, except the man she couldn't stand the sight of, came to see her off. The frailty and illusion of friendship. It wasn't an enviable position to be an outsider in a small town. It took a lifetime to be accepted. There was no belonging to such a place. A person could buy their way into the town, but when people fall on hardship then one comes to understand the brutal reality of friendship.

The driver nodded, "ma'am. Miss. Good day to you." They smiled thinly, climbed into the stage, and sat facing forward. The leather seats were hard beneath them. They listened to the bags being stowed and the stage rocked from side to side as the driver and his assistant went about their business. For the most part, it would be an uncomfortable trip, but at least they were the only passengers.

There was an uttering of a few phrases and the distinct voice of the driver. "Yah."

The stage jerked forward. Her time in Lewisburg was at an end and she couldn't help but feel relieved. The next chapter of her life was about to begin. She watched the town pass behind her. She closed her eyes and sighed as they passed her house. When she opened them, the stage had picked up speed and they were clear of the city limits.

On her lap was a leather valise. Its contents were vast, but it contained a letter. The letter in part said, "*I know about the money Lloyd embezzled. I do not hold you accountable. If you have a mind to return home, send for Rick Cleaver.*" She knew exactly what her father meant. Six months after she received the letter, she convinced her husband to do just that.

CHAPTER 29

The man rode a black stallion. It stood sixteen hands high. Its coat glistened in the sun. Both mane and tail were trimmed short and healthy. The muscles and tendons in its legs were well-defined. Its long neck was muscular, and it maintained a keen look in the eyes. A white stripe ran down the nose. It was a beautiful creature. The stallion possessed speed and staying power. The stallion possessed a wild side that the man had managed to subdue, with great difficulty. It was a one-man horse. Just like the owner, it could be temperamental and moody. Stubborn and unforgiving.

The man was tall and rugged. His features were worn, like saddle leather. There was a toughness to him that one saw in his face, even if he did dress a little fancy. He wore a navy-blue pinstripe suit which was a little dusty and stained with sweat, from some hard traveling. He was in Dickson City, a hundred miles to the north-east of Lewisburg, when word came through. It was time to pay Lloyd Ellery. His business in Dickson City was to remind a mine owner by the name of Taylor Ryan of his options. Either pay back the loan to Mr. Tyler as planned, plus the agreed-upon interest or have an accident. The man in the pinstripe suit was convincing.

Rick Cleaver worked alone. He took orders from one man and that was William Tyler. His work usually consisted of reminding people of their obligations, as per the case in Dickson City, revenge, the recovery of debts, and cold-blooded murder. His boss was a tyrant. His acute business sense and his quest to expand his empire beyond the railway caused him many headaches. The further he spread his tentacles west, the more difficult and ornerier he found his opposition. Cleaver had been kept busy, though most of his time was consumed with travel. He was paid handsomely for his troubles and felt at home in his odd, yet not so rare, field of employ. Men with serious business interests and lots of money at stake had their problem solver. They were usually a grizzled veteran of the war. For it was a lonely job and a man had to be content in his own company if he was going to make some money out of it. He also needed to be rugged and tough. Skills with a gun were welcome but not necessary. A man could learn the rudimentary skills soon enough, but a man who had no experience with death was not a likely candidate for such a position.

Cleaver was always on the clock. He watched people like a hawk does its prey. He had developed into a fine tracker, though it wasn't a skill he was natural at. He was persistent and once set on a course of action, would see the job accomplished. Cleaver had an eye for trouble and a mind for violence. There were times, when he first started, that he felt a certain compassion for those he maimed, extorted, or killed. But he weathered the storm of guilt and soon learned that men and women of all shapes and sizes worked themselves into a position they couldn't get out of. It was their fault and they needed to suffer the consequences. It was of their own doing. There was no one else to blame for the misery that befell them. In life and death situations, some made promises they never could keep. Others pleaded to his conscience and were left staring down the barrel of his Remington into his cold green eyes. They were distant, yet he was tuned in to what was going on around him.

Cleaver was aware of Ellery and his misdeeds. Tyler had always been straight with him in such dealings. His instructions were clear. Kill Lloyd Ellery. However, there was to be a bonus if he antagonized the little man for a while before he pulled the trigger.

Cleaver hitched the stallion out front of the Dusty Boot, dusted himself down, looked both ways along the street and entered the saloon. The bar was nearly empty and a big barkeep with black eyes and a swollen nose moved along the bar responding to orders. He fished in the pocket of his suit for some money and slapped it on the table. His voice was gravelly. "A beer, a bath, a bed, and a woman. In that order. Take what you need and leave the rest."

Marlowe was tired. "Sure thing mister."

"It looks like you've seen better days."

"Yeah, well I ain't in the mood to share my feeling today stranger."

"Fair enough." He left the words hanging, waiting for a reply.

"Marlowe."

The beer was placed in front of him. He took off his bowler hat and ran his hands through his thick dark hair. "Thanks."

Marlowe walked across to the bottom of the stairs and yelled out. "Amy, Rosa."

A minute later they stood at the top of the stairs. They did so with their hands on their hips, demanding to know what he wanted.

Could one of you ladies please take care of the stranger? He needs a bath, a room, and the usual.

Amy looked the man up and down and looked at Rosa. The latter skipped lightly to the edge of the landing and made her way downstairs. The last thing she wanted was to spend another night with Marlowe. He spent all his time bellyaching about what happened. "My name's Rosa. I will run you a bath and then I'll be back directly."

He nodded. "Thanks, ma'am."

It was Marlowe who restarted the conversation. "What's your handle, stranger?"

"The name is Rick Cleaver."

"It is a pleasure to meet you, Mr. Cleaver. Are you just passing through or do you have some business in town?"

"I never go anywhere without a reason, Marlowe." The barman considered himself a good judge of character, and the man appeared amicable enough, but there was a hardness to him. "Yes sir, I reckon you don't."

The bath was lukewarm and though Rosa was company enough, she was distant and aloof.

"I'm looking for a fellow by the name of Ellery, Lloyd Ellery."

Now he had her attention. Over the next two hours, she told and retold the downfall of Ellery and of the events that happened with Langford and Hannon. Of course, she didn't forget to mention Slick Jones. She sat on the edge of the bed and her animation caused him to smile. At first, he considered her a hard woman, embittered by circumstance. He had seen many of them throughout his travels. They turned angry, cold, and vengeful to the world and their place in it. In his experience, it was common. It was only when she finished talking and looked at him with a tilted curiosity did, she realize that she never asked why the man was looking for Ellery.

Her voice was sincere. "Why are you looking for Mr. Ellery?"

"I have known him for a long time. I was in Dickson City when I heard he was in Lewisburg. I got to reminiscing and thought I better stop by and visit my old friend."

Cleaver passed the afternoon and evening away with Rosa. Her company had become increasingly livelier as time passed, but in the end, it was a quiet night. Rosa breathed softly as she slept. Her petite frame was almost obscured by the folds of the blankets. Rick Cleaver lay awake. His mind was on the task ahead. He was a creature of habit and his inquiries had taught him what he needed to know. He knew the names of the lawman and their capabilities. He had learned about the downfall of Ellery and the attempt on his life by the former sheriff. The lawmen were capable and serious about their profession. He would do well to stay clear of them. He smiled, yawned, and closed his eyes.

The night fell heavy across the town. One by one the lights were dimmed and Lewisburg was swallowed by the darkness. The feeling of dread that had sat heavy over the heads of the citizens of Lewisburg remained.

CHAPTER 30

Lonergan had been drowning in his sorrow for days without talking. He found cell life, not that discomforting. He slept and when he wasn't sleeping, he paced the floor. His third option was lying on the bunk staring at the ceiling. He dried out a bit and outside of the influence of his brother and Lloyd Ellery he had begun to think a bit differently about things. He needed to clear his conscience. He was caught square, trying to shoot Ellery, but he wasn't going to let the little man get away with it. His salvation seemed a mite wrong after what he had a hand in, but he knew no other way. He would confess to his sins and let the law deal with him as it saw fit. In the meantime, he had to live with himself as best he could. His fall from grace was obvious and the rumor and innuendo that have accompanied it did not come close to understanding why. He doubted if he would ever know. Still, he had a choice and made it. Remorse loaded with guilt can keep a man's mind occupied. It weighs him down and distracts him from his purpose. It eats away at him and he either swallows it or bites down hard on the feelings it creates. It takes a cold man to ignore it, like a thought that doesn't make sense. But, ignoring it never makes it go away, it just hides for a while until it returns unexpectedly. Men find their way of dealing with it because they all have it. It stems from the deeds and the actions of rash immaturity, anger, or drunkenness. Quite often it is the same method of dealing with it that caused the need to feel such a way in the first place.

Hannon and Jones were talking about the impending nuptials. Sarah and Bertie McGee rode into town earlier that day and she had stopped in at the office to talk with her fiancé, whom she assured they would be having a conversation about his current field of employment.

The door closed and Jones laughed. "No sir. I am not the marrying kind."
"I recall myself saying that a time or two, Slick. But things have a way of finding you. I reckon you will have little say in the matter. I see the way you look at Elsa Thompson."
Slick pushed his hat up with his index finger. "Now you wait…"

He was interrupted by Lonergan. It was like sunshine after rain. "Come on Slick. You have been sweet on Elsa for long as I've known you. If you had any sense about you, you would know that the girl is keen on you too."

The lawmen eyed one another surprisingly before they stood and walked to the cell.

Lonergan rolled off the bunk and approached the cell bars and grabbed them. "Don't let the filly getaway, Slick?"

The sight of the man-caused Slick some mixed feelings. He knew the former Sheriff better than most. He was a good man; he just made the wrong decisions. Then again, perhaps he was always no good. He couldn't work it out. "What is it you want?"

He grabbed hold of the bars. "I'm ready to talk."

Jones looked up at the sheriff and smiled. "We're ready to listen."

Hannon unlocked the cell and decided not to put the shackles on him.

The former sheriff led the way into the office and sat opposite the lawmen, with Jones to his left. In the minute of silence that ensued Jones caught a look in Lonergan's eyes. It was one of regret and deep-seated sorrow. The man was remorseful.

"Where do you want me to start?"

Jones took control of the interrogation. "Were you in cahoots with Ellery?"

You always get straight to the point, Deputy."
He ignored the remark. "Well, were you?"

He nodded. "Yes."

"In what way?"
"The parcels of land he acquired were through force and manipulation. The Cameron spread, the Johnson claim, and the Wilson ranch."

Jones sat on the edge of the desk. "I have no proof of Ellery's dealings with Cameron and Johnson. The legal work is sound," he paused, "and we're willing to move ahead if you claim otherwise."

"I claim otherwise. I was present when Ellery and Will conversed about attending to such matters."

"Where were these," there were a brief pause, "conversations?"

"In Ellery's private room at the Dusty Boot."

"What about Marlowe?"

Mention of the man's name caused him the greatest grief. He had been party to cold-blooded murder, but manhandling his friend the way he did, caused him some discomfort. He would lie to protect him. He owed him that much. "The only thing Marlowe is guilty of is wanting to be liked. Nothing else."

"You and Marlowe are pretty close. Are you sure he played no part in all of this?"

He stared from Jones to Hannon and back again. He saw the look in their eyes but held their gaze. "I'm positive."

Jones and Hannon let that topic slide. "What about Wilson? I have evidence that suggests he didn't die as you claimed he did."
Lonergan was willing to bear all. He had nothing to lose and everything to gain. A clean conscience allows a man to sleep at night. He can walk and breathe without carrying the burden of guilt and shame on his shoulders and in his heart. "I know you have it Slick. It was that which tipped me over the edge. I guess my conscience

got the best of me. I ain't blaming you of course, but I saw the look in your eye, and I knew I let you down."

"Is that so?"

"That's right. Anyway, Will shot Wilson twice in the back and I helped burn down his ranch."

The mention of Wilson's house burning down caused him to intervene. "What happened with Wade?"

"Same as Wilson, only Will was supposed to make it look like an accident."

Hannon shook his head, stood, and paced the floor behind his desk. "What part did you have in my brother's murder?"

Lonergan stood hastily and the chair scraped across the floor. His legs were straight, and he stood firm. Hannon stopped pacing and stared at him. "I had no part in Wade's death. Will was after revenge for what Wade did to him."

The Sheriff raised his voice. "It was justified."

"I know that. I reckon Ellery used that to leverage Will to kill him. He has a habit of preying on the weaknesses of men."
Slick persisted. "Henson told me that if he told anyone about how Wilson truly died, you would kill him. Is that right?"
"I was trying to protect my brother."

His voice was harder. "Is that right?"

"It is."

Hannon took over the questioning. The mention of his brother had stirred some anger within him, but he managed to control himself. "What part did Ellery play in all this?

"He paid Will for killing Wade and Wilson."

Both men became animated. They stared at one another for a long time. The moment had arrived. They knew Ellery was crooked and up to no good.

"Would you be willing to testify in court?"
"I will."

Hannon pushed. "Why?"

Lonergan sat back down and the Sheriff followed suit. "I've done wrong. I haven't always been this way. I was once a prideful man. I took upholding the law as my life's calling, but somewhere along the way, I got lost. Will rode back into town and he formed a bond with Ellery and I just fell into line. I was never strong enough to say no to them. I am not blaming anyone else but myself for the choices I made. I own them. I am trying to right the wrongs of my past. I am not asking for forgiveness, because I will never be able to forgive myself. I owe it to you Hannon and the folks of Lewisburg. I owe it to the family of Wilson, Cameron, and Johnson, but most of all I owe it to you, Slick."

The deputy had been quite pensive. "Why me?"

"You're a good man, Slick Jones. That's a good enough reason for me."

Hannon took out a pencil and paper from the drawer and laid it on the table in front of Lonergan. "Write it all down. Slick stay with him. When he's done make sure he has a bath and a hot meal."

"Where are you going?"

"I'm going to find Ellery and bring him in."

Jones nodded. "Be careful."

Hannon didn't hear him. He removed his Winchester from the gun-rack and exited the office in quick time.

CHAPTER 31

Rick Cleaver raised his right hand and slapped Lloyd Ellery across the face. The man howled in pain and cowered in fright, but on the top floor of his house, there was no one there to hear him. He was in a bind. He had returned to the house only moments earlier. Cleaver had been waiting there for him. The man's presence startled him, but then recognition set in, but before he could speak Cleaver had punched him in the mouth. He fell hard against the floor. He was unconscious for only a moment but that was long enough for Cleaver to tie his hands behind his back.

His voice was pleading. "Rick, it's me, Ellery. I sent for you."

Cleaver spat on the floor. "I never liked you, Lloyd. Ever since Maggie decided she was going to stop having fun with me and marry you, I have waited for this moment."

It was happening too fast and he struggled to make sense of it. "You mean, you and," there was a long pause as he went searching for the words. He had gone back in time, to a place that shaded his memory in black and white images. There was his father-in-law, his wife, their maid, Magda and then there was Rick Cleaver. He was always there. He was his father-in-law's fixer. "She never let me call her Maggie."

Cleaver smiled and backhanded him, and he fell to the floor in a whimper. His face was red, and his lips swollen. Cleaver was enjoying himself.

"Why are you doing this to me?"
"You know why?"

"Rick I," he thought better of playing innocent. "How did he find out?"

Cleaver laughed. "Mr. Russell Becker."

Ellery's head was spinning. "I don't understand."

"The boss's new accountant."

There was a genuine look of confusion in his eyes. He had been painstakingly cautious. The method he used to move the money was ingenious. He was proud of his scheme. Take enough that it adds up to a hefty sum, but not enough to cause suspicion. He had complete control of the finances. It was foolproof, well so he thought. "But I was cautious."

"Not cautious enough. Becker is fastidious, nothing escapes his attention. He explained your scheme to me one day. I can't remember it exactly, but I do recall him saying that you were a creature of habit. Patterns, he said you used patterns."

Ellery knew what Cleaver was saying, even though he didn't go into detail. He hung his head and started to cry. The man called Becker must have gone over years of records. It would have taken time and some ingenuity on the man's part to find the patterns he was talking of.

Cleaver persisted. "Becker said you had an affinity with odd numbers."

"What's to become of me?"

"William Tyler is a serious man, Lloyd. Then again you know that."

"You mean?"

"That's right Lloyd. You're to die."
Where had it gone wrong for Lloyd Ellery? He couldn't work out how he seemed to have it all, that is, respect, money, and opportunity, and in just a mere week he had nothing. Lonergan tried to kill him and he had embarrassed himself by wetting his pants. His wife, which Bernice was a pale imitation of, left him. He was forced to stand down as mayor and he lived under fear of being implicated by the former Sheriff. Tears fell slowly at first, but when he raised his head, he saw the wedding picture of him and his wife on their wedding day. Memories flooded back. Regrets roosted on his shoulders. If he had been patient, he would have inherited the Willian Tyler fortune. It was lust that had brought him undone. The lust for wealth led him to embezzle. The lust for respect and notoriety had caused him to steal and murder. Lust of the flesh led him to Bernice Lonergan. His tears were heavy, and he sobbed. His

words were wracked with emotion. "But I don't want to die."

Cleaver slapped Ellery across the face again and blood ran fast and thick out the man's mouth. "You don't have a say in whether you live or die. You only get to choose how you die. I've been given my orders and I'll see them through."

The force of the blow knocked a tooth out and Ellery spat it out on the floor between them. It landed on the rug and made no sound. He was desperate. "I've got money, lots of it. Take it all, just don't kill me."

"I'm not interested."

"But, it's more money than you've ever earned. You can quit working for Tyler, buy yourself a place, and settle down."

Cleaver was loyal to his employer. Tyler wasn't a great conversationalist but when he spoke people listened. His manner was rough, and his mind was shrewd. Tyler gave people a chance, but no more than they deserved, and the man sniveling before him, had no more chances. He was going to die. His orders were to make the man beg for his life and that is exactly what he had done. He grabbed Ellery by the hair and pulled his head back. He unleashed a series of slaps across the man's face. His skin had shown signs of bruising and Cleaver reasoned that he had suffered enough. He moved across to the window. His stallion was hitched to the gate. People passed, indifferent to the scene unfolding in the upstairs room. A wagon headed for town. A man on a horse passed by at a gait for Darville. Men and women went about their daily obligations without due consideration for the former mayor of Lewisburg. He turned away from the window, but if he had watched for a moment longer, he would have seen a big man, with a grim expression. He held a rifle in his right hand and wore a badge on his chest. He turned the corner and walked up the hill.

Cleaver ignored Ellery's plea. "Money doesn't impress me. Lloyd."

"Please, Rick. What will Margaret think?"

"She won't care."

"She may be upset with me now, but she'll come around. She always had before."

"Well, I suppose there's no harm in telling you."

He was confused. "What are you talking about?

"I'll wager that it was Maggie's idea to send for me."

He recalled the conversation he had with his wife. It was she who recommended he send for Cleaver. "What do you mean?"

"Maggie knew that once she sent for me, your fate was sealed. It was arranged by her father. As soon as Becker discovered the embezzlement, your days on this earth were limited."

"She set me up?"

Cleaver had nothing else to say. He walked around behind Ellery and unsheathed a double-edged knife, with a six-inch blade and a four-inch wooden handle. He kept it in a sheath affixed to the back of his belt. It had proven invaluable several times. Once again, he grabbed the man by the hair and flipped the knife in the air and caught it with the blade pointing down. He raised the knife in his hand and brought it down swiftly.

Ellery lifted his head and watched the man raise his hand. The dull blade, ominous, and life-ending. The point was sharp, and the sun glinted off the blade. A shadow fell across the cold steel. The knife came down and zeroed in on his chest. He heard a voice, a stab of pain, and the echo of a gun. Blood spilled onto him from above as the man who held his head fell.

Rick Cleaver's life was ended by a bullet that hit his right cheekbone, deflected, and came to rest in his neck. He died instantly and careened against the wall and fell to the floor. His killer, Sheriff Thorn Hannon, stood at the entrance to the upstairs room. He could see that the man was dead, but Ellery was still breathing. He fell to the floor, lying on his side.

The lawman moved across to the window and shattered it with the butt of the Winchester. A couple of startled passers-by looked up. He stuck his head through the window. "Someone send for the doctor."

People responded instantly and began to run towards the main street, and he returned to the fallen figure of Ellery.

He blinked rapidly and winced. The pain was great. The knife was embedded in his chest and he bled profusely. He knew someone was there, and he hoped it was his wife, Margaret, but knew it was too late. She had deserted him because he hadn't been the man, she expected him to be. "Who's there?"

"It's the Sheriff."

He blinked rapidly and stared up at the lawman after the latter untied his hands and laid him on his back. "I'm dying."

He went to pull out the knife, and wrapped his fingers around the blade, but was stopped by the wounded man. "Don't."

Hannon looked at him curiously.

Ellery spoke in whispers between gasps of pain. "I don't want you to save me only to hang me at a later time."

"Is there anything you need to say?"

Ellery stared at the ceiling. A numbness consumed him. It started at his feet and worked its way upward. His last words were endemic of the man himself. They reflected his moral self. They were indicative of the man he had become. Three lousy words. Not all men get a chance to utter a passing phrase to the world and those that do generally offer some platitude regarding their life or those he shared it with. Ellery uttered three lousy words. "Why? Why me?"

THE END